EFD1:
STARSHIP
GOODWORDS

Compiled & Edited
by
DONNA & ALEX
CARRICK

**CARRICK
PUBLISHING**

EFD1:
Starship Goodwords
©Carrick Publishing 2012, 2013
Compiled and Edited by
Donna & Alex Carrick
Kindle Edition Published 2012
Print Edition Published 2013

Carrick Publishing
Cover design by Sara Carrick

Print ISBN 13: 978-1-927114-64-3

Kindle ISBN 13 978-1-927114-38-4

CARRICK
PUBLISHING

Table of Contents

Forward, Donna Carrick   5
Family Recipe, Cathy Astolfo   7
Corner Store, Donna Carrick   25
Remember Me, Alexander Galant   45
Stooping to Conquer, Joan O'Callaghan   59
Incompetence Kills, M.H. Callway   71
Family Values, Sylvia Maultash Warsh   77
Giving Thanks, Kathleen Bjorn   81
The Battle of Beavercoat, Melodie Campbell   85
Treasures in the Attic, A.C Cargill   91
Dance, Rosalind Croucher   95
Finding Calm, Sheila Jeffries   97
Murmur, Mike Slater   101
Fostering Humanity Manifesto, Paulissa Kipp   103
Cole's Notes, Melanie Robertson-King   107
Running Parallel, Tracy L. Ward   123
The Minstrel's Spell, Susan M. Botich   133
The Legend of the Corkscrew Swamp,
        Dayna Leigh Cheser   145
The Mighty Pen, Troy Lambert   153
The Predator's Prerogative, Ira Nayman   169
My Wife and I Argue over our Travel Plans,
        Alex Carrick   179
Oh, Okay, and the Good Soldier Schweik,
        John Thompson   187

Foreword

In May of 2012, Alex Carrick had an idea: Why not create a FaceBook Page where authors of all genres would be welcome to post excerpts from any work, and where readers would be invited to explore and discover new treasures?

We called our page the *Excerpt Flight Deck for Readers and Authors.*

Little did we know the exceptional talent our group would attract!

Before long, we were seeing excerpts from a variety of genres, including literary, crime, poetry and blog articles.

Then I had an idea:

Let's invite group members to join us in a series of cross-genre anthologies, designed to offer readers a high quality sampling from a talented mix of authors.

Again, we were astounded by the results.

In this first in our series, *EFD1: Starship Goodwords*, we bring you the best of these contributions, including: Crime Fiction, Flash Fiction, Poetry, Persuasion, Literary Fiction, Paranormal and Humor.

We hope you will thrill to new authors like Catherine Astolfo, Alexander Galant, Joan O'Callaghan, M.H. Callway, Sylvia Maultash Warsh, Kathleen Bjoran, Melodie Campbell, A.C. Cargill, Rosalind Croucher, Sheila Jeffries, Michael C. Slater, Paulissa Kipp, Melanie Robertson-King, Tracy L. Ward, Susan M. Botich, Dayna Leigh Cheser, Troy Lambert, Ira Nayman, Alex Carrick, John Thompson and yours truly, Donna Carrick.

We present these fellow authors with the greatest of pride, and trust you will come to treasure their work as we have.

Yours in the spirit of excellence!
Donna Carrick, 2012

FAMILY RECIPE

Catherine Astolfo

Years after Pom-Pom disappeared, the trunk arrived at my door.

That afternoon I had Skyped the girls—young women, really—who, I can tell, I'm not stupid, are a little frustrated that their mother is still hovering. Their faces satellited in and out of the screen, frozen in cyberspace from time to time, but even through the cosmos I could feel the impatience. After two thoroughly dissatisfying conversations from different parts of the world, I went out and stood on the front porch, shivering, sneaking my last— once again—cigarette. I didn't want any of my coats to give me away by soaking in the smell, so I was freezing to death as I inhaled the final (I swore it was) blessed smoke.

Just as I sucked out the last possible drop of nicotine, a delivery truck slid its way into the fortunately empty driveway and skidded to a halt. At first the cargo resembled a small coffin and I was not sure it was for me. But my formal title was clearly marked on top and once I'd proven my identity to the pimpled delivery boy, he left it in my front hall.

I tried twice to break open the thin wooden bars and façade in which the trunk had been delivered. Deciding to use something more efficient than my hands, I stopped by the bar, filled my glass with vodka and orange juice (the juice because it was still early), and proceeded to the garage.

There I found a crowbar, an item I hadn't known existed in the house of a politician whose hands, to my knowledge, had never even held a hammer. Back at the carton, I hacked away at the veneer until I uncovered a deep brown chest.

Exquisite engravings graced every face of the rectangular box. Beautiful figures in long sinuous gowns, male and female, danced through carved gardens from panel to panel. Their faces were slightly oriental, long hair flowing over shoulders or twisted into buns. Flowers, vines and stems intertwined over the lid and corners. An upturned brass handle, sealed with a rusty combination lock, grinned invitingly. The little trunk stood proudly on four brass claws.

Astonished by the craftsmanship of the trunk, but curious about the contents, I returned to the garage. I once more hunched over with a tool in one hand and a newly refreshed drink in the other. The pliers would not normally be strong enough to crack a lock, but this one was old and rusty and snapped after only a few minutes of muscled determination. A cloud of dust sprang into the air as I lifted the lid, forcing me to gulp quite a lot of my screwdriver in defense.

I got down on my knees and peered into the depths of the chest. It appeared to be mostly empty. A shoebox, a bunch of letters bound together with a withered elastic band, and an old photo album were its only contents. I went for the photos first. New drink in hand, I carried it to my reading chair, switched on the light, and opened it to the first page. And there, in the small black and white images, was my grandfather.

Pom-Pom was a tall, stately man when he was young. His hooked nose made him look rather patrician. I knew from experience that he had sandy flyaway hair and startling blue eyes, but of course these were not apparent in the colourless photos. There were dozens of the little squares, mostly of my father as a baby. It was probably that thing you do with your first child – take pictures of as many poses as you can because you find them so fascinating – and then fail to do with your second. Little did Mary know, of course, that my father would be her only child. Whenever he appeared in the pictures, which was not often (I figured he was likely the photographer), Pom-Pom never smiled. Yet I remember his infectious toothless grin as he opened the door to his suite whenever we visited. Perhaps happiness only came later in life; perhaps he was simply suspicious of human imagery.

Dad never talked about his parents. His mother had died very young, he'd said. He only remembered Veronica, Mary's second cousin, who had raised him without benefit of a man. By the time Dad was old enough to commit memories for conscious retrieval, Pom-Pom was long gone. When Pom-Pom came back into our lives, my father was not interested in a relationship. He and my mother had moved to Toronto and not once did he return for a visit to Ottawa while his father was there. He made me promise that I would have nothing to do with the old man and I swore I would not. However I was far too intrigued to stay away and so began a series of clandestine visits to the YMCA on Argyle with my two little girls in tow. Each time, Pom-Pom would greet us with that sideways smile, eyes dancing, and offer a small surprise for my daughters—a candy or a chocolate—and regale us with stories about his lifetime of adventures. He'd been all over Canada, from the east to the west, he said, and even to the far north. He described his travels in detail, told funny tales about the people he'd met, or had us in stitches (okay, mostly I was the one laughing while the girls wiggled and fretted impatiently) over some of his antics. My daughters, possibly because they didn't see them much, never mentioned these outings to their father or maternal grandfather. Or perhaps they knew, from my nervous and secretive aura, that Pom-Pom was a taboo topic.

Still chuckling at the memories of Pom-Pom's stories, I had just refilled my drink (no orange juice needed; it was getting on in the day) when the telephone rang. Without looking at the call display, I knew who it was. James's secretary usually called around this time. *He won't be home for dinner, they're tackling a sensitive issue, they'll just grab something later, might be very late, he says don't wait up, they'll be holed up at the Brookstreet in some king sized bed...* Okay, so the last part Hillary never said, but I could always sense the apology in her voice. Hillary had to know that James and his personal assistant were having an affair. I know I did.

The only reason he hadn't left me for Elizabeth was his career. James Asquith-Smith was the quintessential squeaky-clean, honest, upright politician whose platform was always full of righteous indignation at the collapse of societal morals. Therefore, despite the fact that he was probably in love with Elizabeth, and no longer had sex with his wife, James would stick around as long as I did. If I left him, he could play the card of being bereft and wronged. So far, however, we were at a standoff. Our daughters were in their first and second years of university respectively, so I had no real reason to stay. I was simply too angry and too selfish to go. James was the one who'd betrayed *me*. Why should I be the one to move out? Sometimes I seethed with my hatred of him; sometimes I grieved for what I had lost. I did nothing around the house. I hired people. I sat and watched films. I shopped. I went to spas. I figured I could hang on longer than he could.

In fact, I found out about James and Elizabeth on one of my many shopping trips. I was in one of those fancy new stores in the Rideau Centre, the kind that have co-ed change rooms. I happened to be standing nearby, fingering a silky blouse I wanted, when Elizabeth Fleming came out of the change room. I was about to wave and say hello when I noticed her face: a strange reddish flush of the cheeks, a slight cat-got-the-mouse smile, radiant eyes. Instinctively I ducked behind the dress racks. Two minutes later, out walked The Honourable James Asquith-Smith, flushed cheeks, victory grin, luminous eyes. Now I knew at last what writers meant when they said your heart squeezed, your stomach flipped, the blood pounded in your head. I felt nauseous because I knew exactly what they had been doing in those change rooms. It was one of the naughty things that James used to like to do with me.

Yes, I had known, really, in that secret part of myself that doesn't like to admit the obvious. The late nights, the missed dinners, the special care he took when he dressed for work, that new cologne. But I'd hoped, I guess, that James might be having a quick fling with someone who didn't really count and therefore wouldn't last. Elizabeth Fleming, however, was dangerous: beautiful, confident, brilliant, witty. I'd actually liked her. It was three years now and counting. Longer than it had taken the Romans to scale Masada, but I was certain that I could hold out longer than the little Jewish community had.

Once I'd murmured my thanks-for-letting-me-know to Hillary, I settled in for a long look at Pom-Pom's old artifacts, actually thrilled that I would have the entire afternoon and night to plow through this adventure alone. The fact that my husband was out screwing someone else, well, I decided to let that go for now. Besides, I had my own screwdriver right here, I joked with myself, and myself found me quite amusing.

Six years ago, my Dad had been killed in a car

accident in Toronto, just two years after Mom died from cancer. So, as an only child, I was pretty much by myself, especially now that the girls were grown up. No one else would be interested in this history, but I'd always found family trees fascinating. Maybe that's because I didn't have much of a one. I was excited by the prospect of finding long-lost relatives. Perhaps I had several aunts and uncles who had passed away and left me hordes of cousins. Maybe one of them was a rich successful lawyer, or even better a private detective, who could get access to the VIP suite at the Brookstreet Hotel.

Unfortunately, the photographs were merely pictures of Pom-Pom and my father and Mary, one after another in very pedestrian poses. Pom-Pom was always slightly out of focus in these pictures, unsmiling, and formally dressed. Perhaps my grandfather had left to tour the country in his grief over his wife's death and had never remarried. In fact, there wasn't one single clue about other possible broods or my lawyer/private eye cousin. And in the few years that I'd known him while he lived at the YMCA, he'd never answered any of my questions. He'd just give me that quizzical, eyebrows-raised, sparkling eyed look and go on with stories about places called St. Louis de Ha! Ha!, Hairy Hill and Pecker's Point.

Bored looking at the same pictures over and over, I reached for the letters. The elastic band snapped in my fingers. I could tell right away that the missives had been written in Pom-Pom's shaky hand, which meant they'd been penned when he was older. They were all addressed to my father and they were all stamped 'Return to Sender', with a post office box as the address. I started to hum the old Elvis song as I refilled my glass. No need to make dinner, so I also grabbed a handful of chocolate-covered almonds and some nuts. I figured I wasn't invading anyone's privacy since Dad is gone, so I opened up the earliest piece of correspondence. There were only two lines, followed by "Love, Pom-Pom". Hmm. It must have been a nickname given to him by Dad, perhaps a twist on Papa. The same two sentences were repeated on every one of the thirty letters: *"I should never have told you. Please forgive me."* What had he told my dad and why did Pom-Pom need forgiveness? When I studied the dates, I could see that the timing matched the years that I'd been visiting Pom-Pom at the Y.

Slightly frustrated now, I reached for the shoebox. Once again, dusty remains forced me to drink a little more than normal in one gulp. There was exactly one piece of thin, yellowing paper inside, rolled up like a papyrus scroll. On the sheet, again in that shaky hand, were nine words: *Florry, I figure you'll know what to do with this.*

Only my dad and Pom-Pom had ever called me Florry. Everyone else stuck with Florence, or resorted to Flo, so the name was reserved for that paternal side. But Florry had absolutely no idea what to do with "this". In fact, I wondered what Pom-Pom even meant by "this". A few photos, letters that repeated the same obscure message, and a cryptic note. How on earth could I know what to do?

I sat in the circle of lamplight, sipped my vodka, chewed on chocolate and nuts, and tried to think. Outside, the sun was beginning to set over the Ottawa River, spilling orange over the carvings on the trunk. Dust motes floated in the rays, causing the figures to appear to dance. I glanced out the window and followed a flock of geese as they wrote across the dusky sky, practicing their V's. Then I studied the chest again.

It sat very stately on those claw feet, its lid thick and heavy, its body a rectangular box. I peered inside once more. A platform of pine or oak had held the small pickings that I'd just been through, but as I gazed at the shelf, I realized that this was exactly what it was: a shelf. Between the bottom and the top, there appeared to be a great deal more space. There must be a false bottom. Once again, I was down on my hands and knees in front of the trunk. I searched the panel of wood with my hand, trying to find a wedge that I could use to pry it up. In one of the corners, I felt a small opening, but I was unable to squeeze my finger inside. This time, I used James's gold-plated letter opener (inscribed with his name and "Congratulations on Your Win!") as a tool, and up popped the thin shelving. I saw a large scrapbook, about twelve by twelve, bursting with yellowing papers and thick items that made it bulge dangerously, and a small plastic recipe box. Very carefully, I lifted the bundle up and out of the trunk, slammed the lid with my hip, and lowered the prizes onto the flat surface. Sitting on the floor, nuts and vodka to calm the excited fluttering of my heart, I began to explore the treasures. I started with the scrapbook first, because I wasn't, at this particular time in my life, feeling very domestic.

On the first page, a newspaper item was affixed to the black surface. Over time, the glue had smeared through the thin parchment and spoiled some of the copy, but I could still make out most of the words and therefore the gist of the story. A tiny black and white picture of a smiling, attractive woman accompanied the column. Mary (O'Reilly) Byrne, wife of Alfred Byrne, had been murdered in her own church. She was a frequent volunteer housekeeper at Sacred Heart, where she swept the floor, cleaned the pews, and dusted the statues. When the priest entered the church that evening, Mary was lying dead on the altar steps, stabbed in the heart. (A good place to be stabbed in the heart, Sacred Heart, I thought, feeling more than a little silly for some reason. I took another sip to fortify myself.) There were all kinds of accolades listed for Mrs. Byrne, which I skipped over because I had no idea who she was and therefore could not feel sorry for the people who had spouted them. Her family had been too distraught to speak to the reporter. The murder had taken place in St. Mary's, Ontario.

The next page was another newspaper item, this one quite small but at least unmarked. "An eyewitness to the case of Mrs. Mary Byrne, murdered on the altar of her own church, Sacred Heart, reported seeing an elderly woman entering the building around the time of her death. We are asking this person to call Sergeant McCallum at police headquarters, as she may be instrumental in assisting with our inquiries."

Page Three was another newspaper item altogether. Nothing more about Mary. This report was from Mission, British Columbia. I couldn't find a date. Mrs. Ruby Lamont had been murdered at a deserted bus stop in the middle of the night. Again, lots of praise was heaped on Mrs. Lamont by the people who had known and loved her, along with confusion as to why she would be sitting at that particular bus stop at that particular hour. It was quite a distance from her home and she had left her husband and children sleeping peacefully, unaware that Mom had flown the coop. *Roooby, don't take your love to town,* I hummed out loud. Curiously, Ruby had been stabbed in the heart, too.

Pages Four, Five and Six were also columns on the death of married women in small towns across Canada. *Why on earth did Pom-Pom own this kind of macabre collection?* Margaret Phelps had died in the field behind her house, just as she was bringing in some corn for dinner. Some place called Delmas, Saskatchewan. The date was listed as June 3, 1963. Vera O'Malley was murdered in Digby, Nova Scotia, walking along a path in the woods near her home. Constance Haynes was killed in Johnson's Crossing, Yukon

Territory, while on a hunting trip. All five women were highly admired by their friends. Every single one's death had so upset her family that they would not speak to reporters. Every one of the deceased had been stabbed in the heart. In all, they had left fifteen children motherless.

I began to have a strange feeling in my stomach that was not helped along by the nuts and vodka. I had to do something. So I switched to red wine and chips and dip and kept reading.

The pages following those newspaper reports held a cornucopia of photos, all of people and places I'd never seen, not all glued in place. Some of the pictures fell out onto my lap. Smiling, attractive women bouncing small babies on their knees, or standing beside toddlers, protective hand on the children's shoulders. Pom-Pom had also kept all kinds of other memorabilia: café napkins, bus tickets, leaves, a feather, a tiny piece of animal fur.

I flipped back to the newspaper portraits of the murdered women. There was definitely a resemblance, I thought—this one in the album could be Constance, this one good old Ruby. But the imagery was so faded and obscure, both in the newspapers and the scrapbook, that I couldn't be certain.

Suddenly I felt compelled to return to the original photo album. I could swear I saw a resemblance to my father's mother in the smiling visage of Mary Byrne. Had Pom-Pom's first wife, my grandmother, been murdered by a serial killer? Had Pom-Pom followed this murderer all over Canada recording his deeds? Perhaps he'd had suspicions but no proof. Perhaps Pom-Pom had taken matters into his own hands and put an end to the culprit. But then I stomped on that fantasy. Pom-Pom's name had not been Alfred Byrne. As far as I knew, he *was* Alfred, but my Dad's last name was Sullivan, so I assumed...

Just then, the telephone rang again. I looked at the clock and sighed. My life was so predictable. Wednesdays at seven p.m. on the dot, my friend Cara—my telephone friend at least, since she and I never get together except by this method—would call. Cara is an enormous woman in more ways than one. She is hugely fat, loud, and completely self- absorbed. She also inherited her father's insurance company, so naturally James and I are insured to the hilt. I can't really explain why I listen to her except to say that my life in the last three years has been *that* boring. We spend two hours at the least on the phone or at any rate, connected by the wire. Most of the time I put her on speaker and did my exercises, muttering uh-huh now and then so she'd know that I was still there. Not that she really cared. Once I'd even taped my responses so I could get ready for one of James's charity events. This evening, however, I plopped back into my chair with the scrapbook on my lap, the chips and dip and bottle of very good red wine from James's cellar on the side table, so I didn't have to move. In fact, I was able to use the speaker method and continue to scrutinize the scrapbook. After a few minutes, however, Cara was frightened out of her mind when instead of uh-huh, I hollered Holy Shit into her ear.

At the back of the scrapbook, I had found six old-fashioned drivers' licenses, passports and social insurance number cards. The pictures showed clearly that Alfred Byrne, Albert Lamont, Allan Phelps, Alan O'Malley, and Alfred Haynes were all the man I'd known as Pom-Pom. The man I had assumed was Alfred Sullivan, my father's biological parent. No wonder my Dad had never wanted to talk about his mom. She'd been murdered. Not only that, I once again could no longer ignore the obvious – my grandfather had been a serial killer.

After I apologized to Cara for swearing so loudly

she'd actually heard it through her incessant gabbing, I let the scrapbook slide to the floor and thought while my friend finished her narrative. How could Dad not have told me? I took my little girls to see this man, for God's sake! (I forgot for a moment that I'd never told my father about those visits.) He had to have known *something* bad. It was the only explanation for the letters "I never should have told you. Please forgive me". A shiver ran down my spine and I twitched, trying to hug myself out of the shock. I pictured my little girls, around eight and ten, sitting in that room with that man. I imagined his twisted grin as he stuck the knife into the hearts of women who loved him and who had borne his children.

It was very dark now and when I glanced up at the picture window, all I could see was my pale face reflected in the glass. Suddenly the quiet house was not so quiet. I heard groans, scrapes and ghouls. A small animal was rustling at the back door. A dog whined in the distance. I plopped back into my chair, pulling the soft throw around me, and stared at the scattered pages on the floor. Sipping my wine, which I now needed rather than wanted, I began to contemplate the enormity of my discovery. It would be easy enough to find my father's birth records. Had he been born David Byrne? Pom-Pom's cousin Veronica had been Sullivan; perhaps Dad had taken her name instead. What would the Right Honourable James Asquith-Smith do if he discovered he was married to the granddaughter of a serial killer? What would this information do to his career? He would certainly still be a media darling, but of a very different nature. The more I drank, the more I thought, the more an idea began to form quite deliciously. Realistically, the media could ruin *my* life too—and I loved my house, my possessions, my privileges, far too much to give them up. Not to mention my girls and how this infamy could stain the rest of their lives as well. Obviously, I had to keep the secret, though it did occur to me that I could use it to threaten James. Give up Elizabeth or I'll reveal my heritage to the world.

Thoughts running wild, I picked up the small plastic box, incongruously marked "Family Recipe". Inside, each of the index cards held one direction, carefully and clearly printed. "How to Make a Perfect Murder" it began. (1) Always have an airtight alibi. (2) Always dress as the opposite gender, in case an eyewitness sees you. (3) Always have your getaway planned. (4) Obtain extremely good fake identification, even if it's expensive. (5) Always use a name close to your original (such as "Al"). (6) Be sure to be the beneficiary of a large insurance claim. (7) Disappear to a small town far from the current one.

This didn't seem like much of a recipe to me, I thought, merely the ravings of a maniac to whom I was accidentally related. Once again, in that secret part of me that has to finally face up to the obvious, I knew what Pom-Pom had meant by, "Florry, you will know what to do with this". I picked up all of the paraphernalia and threw it into the fireplace. I lit a match and watched as every bit of evidence of my grandfather's perfidy curled into ash. Except the plastic recipe box, of course.

My life returned to normal after that, boring, predictable, dissatisfying, but more than comfortable. Spas and shopping, television and telephone, watching cleaners scrub the house or redecorate, waving good-bye and hello again to the geese, following the moods of the river. Until the night the police showed up at my door. Thereafter, my life irreversibly changed.

Ottawa Herald – Thursday, July 15, 2008

Beloved Politician Murdered

Highly celebrated Member of Parliament, The Right Honourable James Asquith-Smith, was found murdered last night at the Brookstreet Hotel, along with his personal assistant, Elizabeth Fleming. An eyewitness, a waiter at the hotel, reported seeing an old man entering the suite around 7:45 p.m. He was stooped but of average height, had long white hair, and wore large glasses. Shortly afterward, the same waiter delivered a pre-arranged room service order to the suite. Finding the door open, he went in and discovered the bodies. The couple had both died instantly from a stab wound to the heart.

A rumour that they were found dead in the king-sized bed has been dismissed. According to several sources, the MP and his PA often used the Brookstreet Hotel for highly sensitive issues. The MP's wife, Florence Asquith-Smith, denied any hints that her husband may have been having an affair. *"Elizabeth and James were strictly business associates,"* she declared. Added their secretary, Hillary Barnes, *"My employers often used the Brookstreet Hotel to work late at night, as it was private and close to both their homes."* The family's lawyer told the media that

Mrs. Smith is distraught and has been sequestered in her home with the couple's two daughters. No further statements will be issued at this time.

Police have assured the public that they will find the man responsible for this terrible, tragic crime. *"Mrs. Asquith-Smith is not a suspect,"* Chief Superintendent Mark Webster said, responding to a media query. *"She was at home on the telephone with a friend."* Cara Miller, daughter of the late millionaire Robert Miller of Miller Assurity, told *The Herald* that she was indeed the friend who was talking to Florence from 7 p.m. to 9 p.m., which removed Mrs. Smith from the crucial time frame. *"Not that my dear friend Flo would be capable of such a thing,"* Ms Miller declared, *"but I know for a fact that she couldn't have done it. She was at home talking to me."* Ms Miller has given several interviews to the media and plans to write a book.

The search for the man responsible for the crime continues. A sketch has been made public. Anyone with information is asked to call Chief Superintendent Mark Webster. Funeral services for the public and the family will be announced shortly.

A short time later, I found a lovely, somewhat similar house on the ocean in Victoria, British Columbia, where I now live my quiet, satisfying life. A small brown chest sits in the front hall in a place of honour. Deep inside, I have placed a new scrapbook with new newspaper clippings and, of course, the small plastic recipe box.

About Catherine Astolfo

Catherine Astolfo is the author of *The Emily Taylor Mysteries*, published by *Imajin Books*. Her short story, *What Kelly did*, published by *NorthWord*, won the *Arthur Ellis Award* in 2012. Catherine's novels have been optioned for film by Sisbro & Co. Inc.

Visit Catherine at her Website
http://www.catherineastolfo.com/
or at her Amazon Author Page

CORNER STORE

Donna Carrick

I've done many things in my thirty-one years. Some good; some falling short of noble.

If there's one deed, or rather 'un-deed' that still fingers the chords of my memory, one oversight I wish I could put right, it would hearken back to a day sixteen years ago in our local convenience store.

To a girl by the name of Angelina Salvaggi.

It's an excuse to say I was only fifteen at the time. Even then, I was no child, not really. In truth, Penelope Canon has never been naïve.

I was fully aware that child needed my help. I just didn't know how to give it.

Aunt Rachel, send me once again to the corner store for milk. Let me go back in time, as if those sixteen years had never happened. Lend me your personal road map, the one that makes you always do the right thing, even though you're half-crazy at the best of times.

Let me do that day again. Maybe this time I'll be a better person.

***

Something didn't feel right.

The store was empty, except for me. It was dimly lit but clean, smelling of fresh bread, candy and a hint of vinegar.

I walked to the back where they kept the milk in tall coolers. At fifteen I was small, still am, in fact, but in good shape. I lifted the heavy bag with ease.

The owner, Sam Salvaggi, would normally be behind

the counter. He lived with his family above the store. A pleasant man – always ready with a smile and a kind word.

There were two doors at the back of the store, near the dairy coolers. The door on the left led upstairs to the family home. The one on the right led into the storage area behind the refrigerators.

As I carried the milk to the front of the store, Sam's eight-year-old daughter, Angelina, appeared. She came through the storage room door on the right of the coolers. I remember wondering what she'd been up to back there.

She was upset. Her eyes were red and she wouldn't look at me, even when I said *hello.*

She walked quickly, eyes down, through the store and out the front door, into the afternoon sunshine.

A few seconds later Sam, a man of mid-to-late thirties, came through the same door. He nodded, not looking at me, and followed me to the checkout counter.

"Good afternoon, Miss Canon," he said, regaining his composure and meeting my gaze. "Lovely day out there."

His smile was friendly if forced, and I put aside my uncomfortable thoughts of his crying daughter.

"It's perfect. Wish it could stay like this all summer."

"How is your Aunt?"

"She's well, thank you."

"Say hello for me. Tell her I'm expecting the new knitting magazine any day now."

My Aunt Rachel loved to knit. Unless you enjoyed being ridiculed at school, you couldn't wear anything she made, but that didn't slow her down. Sam Salvaggi had a standing order for her favourite crafting magazines, and always set aside a copy for her when they arrived.

"I'll let her know."

I paid for the milk. It was a short walk home to Aunt Rachel's house down the street. I took my time, mulling over the encounter. Something nagged at the back of my mind, telling me I should find the girl, ask her if she was all right.

But I didn't do it. Instead I got distracted, as we sometimes do.

"Is that you, Penelope?"

"Yes, Aunt Rachel."

"Good. Dinner's ready. How was school?"

I put the milk away and sat down to one of my Aunt's eclectic meals, this one a strange assortment of undercooked greens and overcooked meat beside a slice of leftover pizza.

Aunt Rachel was no friend of Martha Stewart. On my Aunt's table, presentation took a back seat to convenience every time.

I thought about mentioning the corner store encounter to my Aunt, but I was hungry and the pizza was good, and frankly I forgot.

Shortly after that, Aunt Rachel sold the West End house and we moved to a condo in the East End of Toronto.

I thought about Angelina Salvaggi occasionally. Sometimes I'd dream about her – in a nagging, guilty kind of way. But for the most part I was able to push that memory down into the place where I stored my personal regrets.

Until now, sixteen years later.

It was Saturday morning, and on Saturdays I'd pick up the paper on my way to visit Aunt Rachel at the condo for brunch.

Usually I would cook, badly. We had that in common.

Something about the story made me feel uneasy.

I couldn't put my finger on it at first, but then I

recognized the name in the caption: Salvaggi. It was an unusual one.

The photo alone wouldn't have triggered my memory. After all, the sad but beautiful young woman on the front page of The Saturday Star bore no resemblance to that little girl from long ago.

Once I made the connection, I imagined I saw something familiar in her eyes, some look she'd retained from childhood.

I held the paper out to my Aunt.

"What is it, Penelope?" she asked, taking *The Star*.

"The girl. Do you remember her?"

"Salvaggi…. The name is familiar."

"They owned the corner store near our old house, on Wayburn."

"Oh, yes, I remember. Lovely family. Always had fresh bread and milk. The wife liked to knit." She read the headline aloud. "Daughter returns home to nightmare."

"You remember that home invasion in the West End last week? They didn't release the family name at the time. According to the story, the daughter was in Acapulco with her boyfriend when it happened."

"What a thing! She must be devastated. What was her name again?"

"Angelina," I said.

"She had an older brother, right?"

"Apparently he was one of the victims. Mother, father and brother. Police haven't released all the details, but it sounds like it was particularly brutal."

"Murder always is," Aunt Rachel said. "And to lose everyone… the poor girl."

"Yes."

***

That night I dreamed I was alone in the store. I rang

the bell for service, but no one came. I had a shopping basket full of chocolate bars and Twinkies.

I rang the bell again, frustrated. Looking for the owner, I wandered to the back where they kept the milk. I spied the door on the right, the one that led to the storage area behind the tall coolers.

Suddenly I was tiny, even smaller than I am in real life. I had to reach up for the door handle. I turned it, but no one was in the storage room. The family lived in an apartment above the store, so I went to the door on the left, opened it and called upstairs, hoping to rouse someone.

Still no one came.

In a hurry to leave that disturbing place, I pulled out a twenty and set it on the counter, under the bell. I reached across the counter for a plastic bag, intending to fill it with my purchases.

But when I looked in the basket, there were no chocolate bars, no Twinkies.

Instead, staring up at me, was a head.

My own.

I woke, unable to shake a sense of horror. My inaction years earlier had obviously planted seeds of guilt.

It was too late to help the child Angelina. Whatever she may or may not have suffered back then, those days were gone.

So was her immediate family.

Still, I felt an urge to seek her out. To help the adult, if there was any way I could.

As a private investigator, maybe I could call on my rather tenuous contacts to gather the details the police were holding back.

What good was it having friends on the force if a girl couldn't get the 'inside scoop' once in a while?

It was probably that kind of reasoning that made me so popular with Toronto's finest.

Hell, why stop being objectionable now? I had a reputation to protect.

Detective Darryl Francis answered on the first ring. He sounded tired.

"Got time for lunch today?" I said.

"Maybe. What's it about?"

"I'm hurt, Darryl. Can't I just buy a cop a donut now and then without having my motives scrutinized?"

He didn't laugh. Not everyone gets my sense of humour.

"I'm kind of busy today, Penelope. Is it important?"

"It's about the Salvaggi case."

"Oh."

***

We met at the Courtyard Restaurant in Yorkville. Darryl is fond of Schnitzel and I like the owners, even though it's too much to eat and they bring soft drinks in cans.

I usually get three meals for my money.

"What's your interest in the case?" he asked.

"I used to know the family. Not well. I grew up in their neighborhood. They owned the corner store."

"Have you heard from them lately?"

"Not for years. But I'd like to help the daughter, if I can. She was a nice girl."

He chewed on that for a minute.

Finally he said, "So you're not on tab?"

"No. Just a citizen, hoping to help a former neighbour."

"In that case, I think you should stay out of it."

That caught me off guard, and I looked at him, with noodles dripping red sauce down my chin.

"Seriously, Penelope. If you're not already in it, mind your own business."

I thought again about that little girl. I remembered the way she avoided looking at me, the way she trembled as she hurried out of the store.

I hadn't helped her then.

"I think she needs my help," I said.

"What makes you say that?"

"Because of what you're not saying. I get the feeling she's a suspect."

He looked at the door, a classic "getaway" shifting of the eyes, and I knew I was right. Even though Angelina had supposedly been in Mexico when her family had been murdered, she was being considered a suspect.

While I sucked back noodles, a case was being built against her.

"But she was in Acapulco," I said.

"Penelope, let it go. I can't talk about this anymore."

I knew better than to press him. He hadn't told me anything, hadn't shared any of the details I'd hoped to gather, and yet he'd told me the thing I most needed to know.

Angelina Salvaggi needed my help. Again.

***

The family phone number was listed, but rang without being answered. I guessed it would be too hard for her to stay there, after everything that had happened. More likely she was staying with her boyfriend, Kevin McNeil, but there were too many McNeils listed in the City Directory.

The paper said Angelina worked at an optometrist's office on St. Clair. I narrowed it down to three with easy streetcar access, and found her working reception at the first one, within walking distance of the store on Wayburn.

She greeted me immediately, with only a hint of a smile.

At twenty-four, Angelina was now much taller than I was. In fact, she could have been a model, with her height, lean angles and general poise. High cheekbones and large dark eyes decorated a classic Roman face.

Still, there was a softness about her, despite her slender features.

"Are you Angelina Salvaggi?" I asked.

She looked alarmed, and for a moment I thought she might run away.

"Do I know you?" she asked.

"We used to be neighbours," I said.

"Then you knew my family."

"I did. I'm so sorry to hear about your tragedy."

"Thank you."

When she looked away, I realized she took me for a curiosity-seeker, so I thought I'd better pretend to buy some glasses. In fact, my eyesight is perfect.

"I need some good quality sunglasses. Can you recommend a brand?"

"Your face is small," she said without looking at me.

"Yes. I don't like when the frames are too wide."

"I think I might have something for you."

She went into the back. I thought again about that storage area in the corner store, the one behind the coolers. I had to fight the urge to follow her.

She returned a few minutes later with a *Chanel* frame, perfectly suited to my face. The kind of thing I'd never wear. Too expensive. Far too tasteful for me.

"It's perfect," I said. I looked at the price – $450. Kept a straight face.

"It comes with the case," she said.

"Good." For a moment there, I thought I might not

be getting much of a bargain. But hey, it came with the case.

"Is that all you need?"

"Yes." I pulled out my Visa, hoping and not hoping it would clear.

It did.

"Have a good day," she said.

"Angelina, take my card. I'm a private investigator. If you need anything, give me a call. No charge. I'd like to help a neighbour."

She looked startled. I instantly regretted my boldness. However, as my Aunt Rachel would point out, it's part of me, for better or worse.

In any event, she allowed me to press the card into her open hand.

I think she said 'Thank you', but it was hard to be sure. She was already turning away, and her voice tripped on a sob.

***

Some good deeds are totally selfless. Others, less so.

I'm afraid this one was largely about how it made me feel, and not so much about what I could or couldn't do to help Angelina Salvaggi.

I didn't hear from her for weeks, but during that time I had the sense of a wrong being righted. As if at least one black mark had been removed from my personal ledger of deeds.

By the time she called, I hardly thought about her anymore. My conscience felt absolved, and therefore cleared.

So it was a surprise to hear her voice on the other end of the line.

"Is this Miss Canon?"

"Please, call me Penelope."

I waited. It's a trick I learned awhile back. Don't prompt the caller. Let her tell you the reason for the call.

The seconds seemed to stretch, but finally she said, "I need your help."

We met at a Panzerotti place on St. Clair, near where she worked.

She told me the story leading up to her trip to Mexico. Her parents had been against it. They were a Catholic family with strong ties to the neighborhood Church. They felt Angelina would hurt her reputation by going off with her boyfriend.

"Our last words were angry," she said. "I felt they never let me have any fun. Now I can't stop thinking about it. I loved them, you know."

Guilt. Something I could relate to. If possible, I felt even more sympathetic to Angelina knowing she had regrets of her own to live with.

"We all say and do things we're sorry for. No one would think you didn't love them, just because you had an argument. The timing is unfortunate, but...."

"The police think I arranged it all."

The words were dispatched without inflection, emotionless. Even her voice sounded disconnected, like the electronic voice that tells you the subway doors are about to close.

I looked at her, a thought worming its way into my mind. I tried to stomp on it, but it squirmed anyway.

Never being one for subtlety, I said, "Why do they think that? I mean, you were out of town."

She thought for a moment, and when she spoke her voice was back to its usual soft, sad timbre.

"I'm not sure why. But I could tell they thought so. They questioned both me and Kevin. They went easy on him, but when it came to me they were pretty harsh."

"What do you need me to do?"

"Well, I was hoping you could ask some questions around the neighborhood. I don't think Kevin or I should be seen doing that. But you could. You never know — maybe you'll find out who did this to my family."

"So we could bring the killer to justice."

"That's right. And clear my name. So the police will know it wasn't me."

She moved her folded pizza around on her plate.

"I have money," she added.

"I wouldn't charge you."

"That's very kind."

She met my eyes directly then, for perhaps the first time, as if trying to study my motivations.

"I remember you," she said slowly.

"From the store."

"Yes."

Something about her eyes told me she remembered not only me, but that day as well. And that she understood, at last, why I felt I owed her.

"So you'll help me?"

"I'll do my best."

But I already wondered how much help I'd be to her. Something felt wrong about the whole thing.

Why would the police suspect a grieving young woman who'd been out of town at the time of the murders?

She didn't look like an addict, didn't behave as if she had no morals.

She was a nice girl, to all appearances — raised on Holy Wafers and family.

My early sojourns to the neighborhood were unproductive. Everyone was horrified about the home invasion that had occurred in their midst. People were watchful, suspecting each other.

The community threw its support behind the sad young woman who'd lost her family.

The third time I rode my bike to Wayburn, I parked it outside our old house and walked up the street to the store. The sign still said Salvaggi's Convenience, but it needed fresh paint.

A group of teenagers were smoking in the small lot beside the store. They looked like young people in any urban centre – lean and mildly intimidating – but I knew from experience these were good kids. They snuck a smoke around the corner from time to time, but didn't dare get up to any great mischief, aware of being watched by neighborhood Nonnas who knitted on porches up and down the streets.

On a whim, and feeling youthful in my skimpy leather bomber jacket and biking boots, I decided to join them.

I pulled out my card by way of introduction, handing it to the biggest boy.

"My name's Penelope Canon. I'm investigating the crime that took place here a couple of months ago."

"You're a Private Eye," he said, handing my card to the next kid. "Cool."

"Do you guys hang here often?"

A general shifting of eyes and shuffling of feet.

"Sometimes. Not all the time."

"What about on March tenth? That was a Saturday."

"Yeah. We were here. But we didn't see anyone strange. We talked about it afterward. Nothing happened while we were here."

"What time did you stay till?"

"The store closes at nine-thirty. We usually hang till around ten."

"But that was a Saturday," another boy said. "We stayed till ten-thirty."

"That's right."

"Did you see anyone in the family that day?"

"Just the father. He was working the store. We went in for pop around nine."

"Did he seem normal?"

"Yeah. He was his usual self. A nice guy. The whole thing really sucked."

"Did the police question any of you?"

The five boys looked at each other before shaking their heads. The big guy said, "Nah. We didn't see anything that would help. Otherwise we'd've told them."

"What about the daughter?" I let that hang, allowing them to interpret the deliberately vague question however they chose.

More shuffling of feet.

"She was in Mexico," one of the boys said.

"With her Inglese boyfriend," another added.

One of the boys snorted.

"What do you think of him?" I asked. I was taking this purely on instinct.

"Her father didn't like him, that's for sure."

"Neither did her brother."

"Had they been seeing each other long?"

"Nope. Only since she dumped Jimmy right around Christmas time."

Wait a minute. Jimmy?

"Who's Jimmy?"

"Jimmy Leone. He was engaged to Angelina for three years. Then she dumped him and started going out with the English prick."

"How'd he take it? Was there any bad blood between them?" This was getting interesting.

"Like a lamb," the oldest boy said. "He never made any trouble. Anyway, her family and his were close. They pushed her to get back together with him."

"She didn't deserve him," the only girl in the group said.

"Jimmy's a saint."

I thought it might be a good idea to track down Mr. Leone.

***

Jimmy Leone pulled a deck chair off the stack and placed it near his own – too close for comfort. I moved it a few feet away before sitting.

I looked up in time to see a hint of a smile.

He was full of muscle and energy. Blue eyes couldn't help their sparkle, despite the circumstances of our meeting.

I would not have described him as a saint.

A god, perhaps, but not a saint.

The kind of guy who could sell corn to farmers in Kansas. So long as they were women.

He looked to be around twenty-eight, only a few years younger than me. A fact that wasn't lost on me.

"They tell me you and Angelina were engaged." I threw that out with my usual subtlety.

"By-gones. Still, I feel bad for her. She didn't deserve that."

I studied his face, the perfect blend of sorrow and regret.

"Have you seen her since you broke up?"

"Once in a while we'll bump into each other. In the neighborhood. Other than that, no. We've talked a couple of times on the phone. I saw her at the funeral."

"So you'd say you're still friends?"

"Yeah, I'd say so. Like I said, I felt badly for her."

"You seem like a nice guy, Jim. Why'd she dump you?"

His eyes turned cold. "We went our separate ways."

"I heard she dumped you for another guy," I persisted. "Some English prick."

"Hey, it's her decision. And anyway, I wouldn't call him a prick."

"What would you call him?"

The smile returned. "I don't know. Maybe a *sciocco*."

I wracked my brain for my half-remembered Italian phrases from when I lived in Little Italy.

"A fool. Why?"

"Because he doesn't see it coming."

"Like you didn't see it coming?"

"Maybe."

The porch door opened and a middle-aged lady stepped out. She saw me and decided, out of politeness, to use English.

"Jimmy," she said, "Angelina just called."

"Ok, ok, I'll be right in." He looked alarmed, as if this was an unexpected revelation he would have preferred to avoid.

"No need to get up. She said to tell you she'd be here around six as usual."

As usual? What did that mean?

And suddenly it hit me. Just like that.

"She's leaving Kevin, isn't she. That's what you meant by *sciocco*. You and Angelina are getting back together."

He waved a hand, as if the answer was irrelevant. "Our families were friends, that's all. Anyway, you'll have to excuse me." He stood, his patience having reached its limit.

"Did it ever occur to you, Jimmy, that maybe Angelina has a thing for *scioccos*?"

"Get the hell out of here!"

"I'm going, Jimmy. But just so you know, I think you've been played, just like Kevin."

I turned to go, was about to plant my foot on the first veranda stair when I felt more than saw him lunge toward me.

Just in time, I jumped off the veranda, my ankle twisting slightly, but protected by the sturdy leather boot. In that instant I avoided his grasp.

I knew I couldn't outrun him, but tried anyway. Within seconds he would reach me, but I had to give it a shot.

As he grabbed my forearm, I spotted the group of teenagers on a porch across the street.

"Hey guys!" I called out.

"Penelope, how's it going?" the biggest kid said.

"Not so good. I need you guys to walk me to my bike."

Before he let go of me, Jimmy turned me to face him.

"We're not done," he said. His charming mask was gone, and in its place was the real face of Jimmy Leone, the lion, the hunter, the man of rage who'd slaughtered the Salvaggi family in cold blood.

Why?

Because she'd asked him to. Angelina, the angel of death. The little girl who despised her family with cause, with an unrelenting hatred. The woman bent on destruction.

"You are, Jimmy. You and Angelina. You're both done."

He released his grip and strode back to his house, to his mother, to the life he'd thrown away.

The kids walked me to my bike, smoking and laughing, innocent of knowledge.

But I knew. And I could never again pretend I didn't.

***

My Aunt Rachel has a saying: It'll all come out in the wash. And so it did, in its own way.

Angelina could have carried it to her grave, but Jimmy was not made of such stern stuff. His temper got the better of him under close questioning by Toronto's homicide detectives, and the truth came barreling out.

Angelina hated her father. By extension, she hated her mother and brother as well. She could never be free, as long as they were alive.

They had millions in savings squirreled away, and wouldn't part with it. They wouldn't even consider helping their daughter get a good start in married life.

All she'd asked for was enough to make a down payment on her own house, a house she and Jimmy could share.

The old bastard was as tight-fisted as he was perverted.

Then she came up with a plan.

She and Jimmy pretended to be through. She took up with Kevin, the Inglese idiota, and a few months later planned a trip to Mexico with him.

This was to be her alibi.

Meanwhile, Saint Jimmy was known throughout the neighborhood to have taken the breakup "like a lamb". His own good nature was his alibi.

Sometime after 2 am, he called the Salvaggi home to say he'd heard from Kevin about an emergency situation in Mexico involving Angelina. Mrs. Salvaggi was frantic. Jimmy promised to come right over and tell them the news in person.

They let him into their home without hesitation.

The lion in lamb's clothing.

About Donna Carrick

Donna Carrick is the author of *The First Excellence* (winner of the 2011 Indie Book Event Award), *Gold And Fishes* and *The Noon God*, available in both paperback and e-book. Her Crime Anthologies, *Sept-Îles and other places* and *Knowing Penelope*, are available for e-readers.

Over ninety thousand copies of her e-books have been downloaded worldwide.

Visit Donna at her Website
http://www.donnacarrick.com/
at www.CarrickPublishing.com
or at her Amazon Author Page

REMEMBER ME

Alexander Galant

Author's Note: This was my entry for a short story challenge. Writers were assigned a specific genre, subject and character and had to use all three in their short story with a 2500 word limit.

I was assigned: Genre: Mystery, Subject: Pen pals, Character: a ten-year-old child. Final word count: 2369.

Dear Pen Pal,

My name is Noah. I've never written a real letter before. I'm 10 years old. I'm in grade 5 and I live in Toronto. I like video games and chess. I have a cat named Zeus, who sleeps in my room.

What's your name? How old are you?

Your pen pal, Noah

***

Dear Noah,

I already know all about you. Don't you remember me?

Have you learned to swim yet? Or are you still afraid of water?

Your friend, Eddie

P.S. What happened to your black cat, Hades?

***

Dear Eddie,

I don't remember knowing anyone named Eddie. I did

know a Freddy once but that was my neighbour's dog. How did you know I had a cat named Hades? He died three years ago when I was 7. He was very old for a cat. We got Zeus a year ago.

When did you know me? I don't recognize your address. And I still don't like the water. I take showers instead of baths. How did you know?

Noah

***

Dear Noah,

I told you. I know all about you. I know you were always afraid of dark. You would wet the bed if you woke up and it was dark. I know you don't like your new mother and hate your father for replacing your real mom.

We used to be best friends. You used to tell me everything. Do you remember me now?

Your friend, Eddie

***

Eddie,

You're freaking me out! How do you know so much about me? I don't hate my new mother, she's nice to me. I don't remember my real mother. I don't know anything about you. I really don't remember you. I'm sorry. Do you have a picture you could send? Maybe I'll remember that way.

Noah

***

Noah,

I'm very upset that you don't remember me. It's your new Mom's fault. She's not nice. She made you forget me. She never liked me. It's because of the accident. That's why you can't remember. Go ask Doctor Zelenko. He would remember me.

Your best friend, Eddie

***

To: Eddie,

Accident? What accident? But - the name doctor Zelenko sounds familiar. It also sounds like a bad guy in a Bond movie. How do I find this doctor to ask him?

Noah

***

Dear Noah,

Check your Dad's address book. He'll have the phone number there. You can find the number there and then you can call Doctor Zelenko. He'll tell you all about me.

Your best friend, Eddie

***

To: Eddie

I've looked but I can't find any address book anywhere. Just tell me the number, or tell me how we first met. Maybe I'll remember then.

Noah

***

Dear Noah,

Do I have to think for you all the time? The address book is in your dad's laptop computer. The password is your birthday. At least it used to be. If not, try your new mom's birthday.

Your only friend, Eddie

***

EMAIL

From: Joseph Thompson

To: Dr. E. Zelenko

Subject: Eddie

This is Noah Thompson's father, I'm following up on the three voice-mail messages I left for you. I caught my son breaking into my laptop. After some prodding, I found out that Eddie may be back. At least I think it's him. He's been communicating with my son via some pen-pal program that the school has started. How could this happen? He's starting to manipulate Noah like last time.

***

From: Joseph Thompson

To: Dr. E. Zelenko

Subject: RE: Eddie

I haven't heard back from you and I'm concerned with Eddie being back in Noah's life. We have to do something about it. I'm worried about Noah and that he might remember what happened.

***

From: Joseph Thompson

To: Dr. E. Zelenko

Subject: RE: Eddie

This is my third e-mail to you. I need you to get back in touch with me. I demand to see my son's file, or else I may have to do something drastic.

***

DOCTOR MURDERED! POLICE QUESTION A PATIENT'S FATHER

(Staff Reporter)

The body of Dr. Eduardo Zelenko (51), of the Hillhome Clinic was discovered this evening by his office security staff after an alarm was triggered. Police are treating the suspicious death as a homicide, citing evidence of foul play and an arson attempt. However, the Fire Marshall believes that the fire extinguished itself because no accelerant was used to start the fire.

One specific patient's file seemed to be deliberately set aflame and left unattended. Police speculate it was burned to destroy evidence of foul play. The patient's father, who allegedly made several attempts to contact Dr. Zelenko and left hostile voice messages is being questioned by police. A small trail of blood outside the scene of the crime was discovered by investigators.

Police are not able to comment on whether the blood found belonged to the suspect in custody or to the victim. No charges have been laid as of yet, but the investigation is ongoing. Since the patient involved is a minor, authorities are withholding all names for the child's protection.

***

EMAIL

From: Dina Thompson

To: Gerald Parker, Principal

Subject: Noah & pen pal

Dear Mr. Parker,

I'm sure you've heard rumours that the police are holding my husband on suspicion of murder.

You know my husband and he would never harm anyone. I was wondering if you could be of assistance. Has Noah mentioned anyone named Eddie?

They have been communicating through the school's pen-pal program. Noah's pen pal is 'Eddie' and an Eddie is no stranger to our family. We went to great lengths to keep Eddie out of Noah's life. When we signed the permission slip for Noah to take part in the pen-pal program, we assumed it was to correspond with a student who lived overseas. I'm not sure how it's possible, but Eddie or someone claiming to be Eddie appears to be taking advantage of the program. I was wondering if you knew who might have had access to the pen-pal addresses. Someone might be using the pen-pal program to pose as Eddie and is using the late Dr. Zelenko's file on my son for background. Any information could be helpful to the police to find this person pretending to be Eddie. Thanks!

Dina Thompson

***

From: Gerald Parker, Principal

To: Dina Thompson

Subject: RE: Noah & pen pal

Dear Mrs. Thompson,

I can sympathize with you and your family's dilemma. However, I am perplexed. Our school fully intended to take part in the pen-pal program but it was cancelled due to the constant threats of a postal strike this year. We did not wish to disappoint the students, so we decided to postpone it until their letters could be sent and received with more certainty. I have no idea who this Eddie is or how he was able to contact Noah, but it certainly was not through our school. If I should learn anything new I will certainly contact you. Best of luck.

***

Dear Noah,

You haven't responded to any of my letters. You can't ignore me forever. If you don't answer, I'll do something nasty.

Your best friend, Eddie

***

> MISSING - A one-year-old white male cat with blue eyes. Answers to the name 'Zeus'. REWARD if found. Dina Thompson 555-7396

***

Dear Noah,

Zeus is a pretty cat. Not as pretty as Hades was, certainly not as smart. If you want to see it again, you should write back to me now.

Your friend forever, Eddie

***

Eddie,

Don't hurt my cat! Please! I'll do anything you want. Just give me back my cat, please!

***

Dear Noah,

I'll be happy to give Zeus back to you. But first you have to kill Dina! She's not your real mom! It's her fault you don't remember me. She's the one who really killed Dr. Zelenko to cover up what he did to you. And now your dad is going to jail for what she did. She has to pay for what she did. Your dad keeps a hunting gun in the garage. The bullets are locked in the metal toolbox. The keys are in your dad's desk - bottom drawer. Do this and you'll see Zeus tonight.

Your best and only friend, Eddie

***

Eddie,

You're crazy! That's murder! I'm not a murderer! No! I can't! I won't do it! Never!

***

Dear Noah,

Dina's not your real mother. She's taken all the pictures of your real mother and put them in a box in the garage. If you don't believe me go look... it's in the shelves next to where the gun is kept. There are pictures of her holding you when you were a baby. But Dina made you forget her... and forget me. Just outside the garage you'll find Zeus' collar. There is a little blood on it. He isn't hurt too badly... yet. He sure yowled when I cut him! If you do what I say, I promise you will see Zeus again. You have to do it tonight!

Your only friend,

Eddie

***

(9-1-1 INCOMING CALL - TRANSCRIPT)

OPERATOR: 9-1-1 What is the nature of the emergency?

FEMALE VOICE: I've been shot!

OPERATOR: Is your address 1366 Stevenson Street?

FEMALE VOICE: Yes, hurry! I'm bleeding badly.

OPERATOR: I have sent dispatch! The police and ambulance will be there shortly.

FEMALE VOICE: (mumbled sound)

OPERATOR: Is there anyone there with you to stop the bleeding?

FEMALE VOICE: Yes... no!

OPERATOR: Ma'am, Is assailant still in the house with you?

FEMALE VOICE: I don't know.

OPERATOR: Do you know who shot you?

FEMALE VOICE: It was... No... it was Eddie.

OPERATOR: Who is Eddie?

FEMALE VOICE: (no response)

OPERATOR: Ma'am? Are you still there?

***

WOMAN MURDERED IN HOME!

Staff Reporter

Local resident, Dina Thompson (36) was found without vital signs in her own home last night. Emergency Medical Services and the police were dispatched to her home on Stevenson Street after the victim placed a call to 9-1-1 shortly after 9:00pm. Police searched the premises and found a 10-year old boy hiding in the garage, crying as he cradled a dead cat in his arms. He could be heard screaming, "Eddie broke his promise!" The boy has been put into the care of child services while police continue to investigate and search for someone named "Eddie" who has been named a person of interest.

In a bizarre twist of fate, the victim was the wife of Joseph Thompson who is still in police custody in relation to the mysterious murder of Dr. Zelenko earlier this week. It is not known if the two cases are connected. Forensics have identified Mr. Thompson's blood near the body of Dr. Zelenko, placing him at the scene of the crime. However, an insider revealed that Mr. Thompson does not have any injuries or marks on his body that would leave a trace of blood. Police say Mr. Thompson has been very cooperative and was visibly upset when learning of his wife's death. However, he refused to answer any questions regarding 'Eddie'.

***

Dear Noah,

I didn't break my promise! I promised you'd see him again. I never promised 'alive'.

Now that your fake mother is dead, do you remember me?

Your best friend, Eddie

***

Yes Eddie! I remember you now! You are not my friend! Leave me alone!

***

(Written on the wall of Foster home - manic writing, carved in with pen)

Dear Noah,

I can't leave you alone! You need me. Now more than ever! Who else will take care of you? You can't hide from me. I am here in this house. I know where to find you.

Your best friend, Eddie

***

(Scribbled underneath in different handwriting)

You are not my friend Eddie. I'm going to go where you can never follow me!

***

(9-1-1 INCOMING CALL - TRANSCRIPT)
OPERATOR: 9-1-1 What is the nature of the emergency?
MALE VOICE: The boy tried to kill himself! We need an ambulance right away! Hurry!

***

PATIENT FILE - CASE NUMBER 612-36

Patient's Name: Noah Thompson

Age: 20

Therapist: Dr. de Winters

Subject, Noah Thompson is currently undergoing treatment for Multiple Personality Disorder. The individual known as "Eddie" was originally an imaginary friend of Noah's when he was three years old. Though not uncommon and generally a normal stage of development for children around the age of three or four, it is also normal for children to create playmates when they feel lonely or do not know how to relate to their parents or vice-versa. It also allows an expression of creativity and healthy fantasy. It only becomes a concern when the imaginary friend prevents the child from interacting or making real friends. Such was the case of 'Eddie' who continued to be a constant presence in Noah's life. We can assume it is a defence mechanism triggered by a boating accident that resulted in the death of Noah's natural mother as she tried to save Noah's life.

The imaginary friend eventually manifested himself in physical form as an alternate identity, when Noah was six and the father began courting Dina Rivers, who later became his second wife. Noah withdrew into himself and 'Eddie' (the persecutory personality) began to act out with hate within Noah, dominating his physical form and retaliating with self-mutilation. The boy's psychiatrist Dr. Zelenko commenced extreme electroconvulsive (shock) therapy treatment, along with medication.

Noah seemed to have responded well to the radical treatment and for three years continued developing normally without incident. During his tenth year the persecutory suddenly resurfaced as an imaginary 'pen-pal'. It is not clear why the dissociative identity of 'Eddie' resurfaced or what triggered it, but one thing is certain: Noah Thompson is still not aware of his actions when he is Eddie.

While undergoing a treatment of medication and therapy, Noah corresponds repeatedly with Eddie, now back to an 'imaginary friend' status. With crayon and paper he continues to relive the traumatic events of when he was ten.

On-going medication, close supervision, and indefinite treatment is necessary.

***

Dear Pen Pal,

My name is Noah. I've never written a real letter before. I'm 10 years old. I'm in grade 5 and I live in Toronto. I like video games and chess. I have a cat named Zeus, who sleeps in my room.

What's your name? How old are you?

Your pen pal, Noah

About Alexander Galant

Alexander Galant *(Remember Me)* was awarded 'Finalist' in the International Book Awards 2012 for his novel: *Depth of Deception (A Titanic Murder Mystery)*. Alexander has also written and directed several short films which have won awards in festivals around the world, including the Silver Remi (Suspense-Thriller) for *The Missing Piece.*

Visit Alexander at his Website
http://www.alexandergalant.com/
or at his Amazon Author Page

STOOPING TO CONQUER

Joan O'Callaghan

Even up in the projection booth, I could see the worried look on Melissa Casaubon's face.

Understandable. *She Stoops to Conquer* was just one week away from opening. Theatre critic Harley Craddock would be in the audience and that could be Melissa's big break. Our local summer theatre, Straw Hat, was just a stepping stone for her. Who knew where a favourable review from Harley would lead? Directing at Stratford? Niagara-on-the-Lake? New York?

Truthfully, everyone was on edge and it wasn't just because of Harley Craddock. Lisa Moncrieff playing the part of Kate Hardcastle, flubbed her lines once again. Melissa turned, caught my eye and nodded. I leaned over and whispered the line into the mike. Lisa looked confused for a moment and then repeated what I'd said.

Walking home after rehearsal, Lisa was quiet. Finally, she spoke. "I don't know what's wrong with me, Penny. I've never had trouble remembering my lines before. I played Rosalind in *As You Like It* last winter and never missed a cue. Now I can't remember my lines, I get dizzy on stage, and nauseous —" Her voice trailed away.

I nodded sympathetically. I'd seen her in *As You Like It*, as I'd seen her in most everything. After all, we'd grown up together — elementary school, high school, and now university. I was at York too — majoring in English. Lisa was in Fine Arts — drama. Both of us were involved with

Straw Hat. Lisa on stage and me behind the scenes.

Lisa was a great favourite and for good reasons. She was majoring in theatre and she was pretty. Long blonde hair, blue eyes. A real ingénue. Just right for the part of Kate. *She Stoops to Conquer* was our second production of the season. Our first had been *I'll Be Back before Midnight.* Lisa played Jan.

The problems actually began to appear in that production. Lisa was stumbling over lines, forgetting some. It was out of character for her, but I guess it was okay because Jan is supposed to be recovering from a nervous breakdown, so the audience just thought it was part of her mental state. And truth be told, she wasn't all that bad. Things had deteriorated since then.

"Probably all you need is a good night's sleep," I said. "We've been at it pretty steadily since the season began. You're just stressed out."

She shook her head. "Don't think so. I've been in lots of productions and never felt any stress other than some jitters when the curtain goes up. I'm not sleeping very well. I take gravol for my stomach and it's supposed to knock you out too, but nothing helps. I don't sleep and my stomach is still upset."

"Why don't you talk to your doctor?"

"Because he'll just tell me the same thing. Get some rest – it's just stress."

I shrugged. "Well, then, try yoga or something like that. It'll help you concentrate."

At rehearsal the next day, nothing was right. The paint the stage crew was using on the sets was the wrong colour, and in one of his more exuberant moments, Larry Dubeau, who played Tony Lumpkin, managed to break a vase that was one of the props. We were already incorporating whatever we had in the way of props, costumes and makeup into our rehearsals. Lisa looked garish in her stage makeup, the rouge and eye shadow accentuating her pallor.

Melissa called time and we took a break. I came down from my perch up in the projection booth and followed her outside. Melissa lit up a cigarette and was quiet for several moments.

"Penny," she said, "how well do you know the play?"

"I know it pretty well," I said with some hesitation. "I've been at all the rehearsals and I have to follow the script. Why?"

She took a long drag on her cigarette and swept her other hand through her cropped grey hair. Then she turned to face me. "If necessary, could you play the role of Kate? I don't know what's wrong with Lisa but she can't seem to get a handle on the part and I can't risk her constantly missing cues and flubbing lines on opening night. Not with Harley Craddock in the audience," she added grimly.

"I suppose I could do it if I had to. Let's hope it won't be necessary."

I walked home by myself, mentally running over Lisa's lines and picturing her moves. My copy of the script had all the blocking marked down so I knew exactly where and when characters were supposed to move on stage. If Lisa couldn't get it together in time for opening night, there was no question that I was in line to understudy her. Stage managing meant that I was constantly immersed in the script.

I was at rehearsal early the next day. I had the crew up on ladders positioning the lights - lekos, fresnels, and gels, and I was in the projection booth giving instructions over the mike. Although, we would have a full technical rehearsal a couple of days before the dress rehearsal, Melissa wanted to make sure the lights were in the right places and not casting shadows over the actors.

Rehearsal was no better than it had been on the previous nights. I could hear Lisa stumbling over her lines. I was busy cuing Bill who was on the lighting board, and running through the lighting for the first time, when I heard Melissa shouting my name. I ran down to the stage. Melissa was on her feet, her hands clenched and shaking the script at Lisa who was in tears.

"What the hell's the matter with you? We're a couple of days away from opening and you're getting worse, not better. By now you should know what you're doing. Now move. You're supposed to be centre-stage, not off to one side."

"I can't," Lisa sobbed. "The lights are hurting my eyes."

"Since when? You've been under lights before. This is nothing new. Come on," Melissa tried cajoling her.

"Let's take a break," she said, finally. "Penny, stay with Lisa. Maybe you can get her focused."

I took Lisa's arm and led her backstage to the dressing rooms. "Here." I handed her a bottle of cold water out of the cooler. "Your makeup is running. Crying's making it worse. I'll touch it up before we go back out. Do you want to run through the next scene before we start?"

Lisa twisted the cap off the bottle and took a long swig. "I just want to relax for a few minutes. Why are we doing makeup so soon anyway? We usually don't do makeup until dress rehearsal."

"Because Melissa needs to see how everything looks under the lights in case something has to be changed."

"Isn't that what the tech and dress rehearsals are for? Why can't we wait?"

I shrugged. "You know how it is. She's all wound up about Harley Craddock being in the audience. She wants everything perfect. This could be her big break."

"What about me? I don't want to look like a fool in front of him. Why is she stressing me out like this? Just because she wants to look good in front of him."

"C'mon," I said. We've only got a couple of minutes left. I'm gonna fix your makeup now."

She sat quietly while I reapplied foundation, rouge and eye shadow.

Melissa called for us to start again. I went back up to the projection booth and watched thoughtfully while they did the second act. Somehow Lisa made it through and Melissa let her go without stopping her.

When rehearsal ended, Lisa shot out the door. I took my time, noting some minor changes in the lighting and then cleaning up backstage. I made sure all the props and costumes were stored. I was sorting the makeup when I heard something behind me. I whirled around and there was Darren Fraser lounging against the doorway. Darren played Marlow, Lisa's love interest in the play. My throat went dry, as much from his nearness to me as from being startled. Darren always had that effect on me. I quickly shut the makeup case and ran my hand through my short dark curls.

"Hi." He flashed that thousand-watt smile. "I was looking for you."

"Well, you found me."

"Yeah. I was just talking to Melissa. She said if Lisa can't pull herself together, you're going to play Kate. "

I looked at him. "I sure hope it doesn't come to that."

"I don't want this thing to get screwed up. Why don't you come an hour early tomorrow and we can have a run-through, just you and me. Before Lisa gets here – so we don't upset her."

I hesitated and then said, "Okay."

I hurried home. I spent the next morning memorizing lines. I already knew most of them. Darren was at the theatre when I arrived. We did a quick read-through. He only had to correct me a couple of times. Then we read the lines and walked through the blocking at the same time. I was pretty confident with that because I'd seen it so often from the projection booth.

We still had a bit of time before the rehearsal was supposed to start, so Darren suggested we grab a sandwich. I was walking on a cloud. Me and Darren Fraser. I felt my stomach do a flip-flop.

We took our sandwiches and soft drinks and found a convenient bench. Darren casually draped his arm across the back of the bench behind me. "What do you think is wrong with Lisa? I've been in other productions with her. She's never had problems like this."

I shook my head. "Don't know. Maybe stress. "

"She's no more stressed than the rest of us."

"Lisa's a perfectionist."

Darren looked at his watch. "C'mon. Time to go in."

That night was the technical rehearsal, so we didn't focus on anything else. I suggested to Melissa that the cast should be in full makeup and costumes anyway, so we could see the total effect. I noticed that Lisa was moving with some difficulty. She held onto the backs of chairs and sat listlessly when I applied her makeup. When I asked her how she was feeling, she just said she was tired. She'd stayed up late working on her lines.

Darren was waiting for me again. I had to put everything away first, and then we walked home together. "You know," he said to me. "You're pretty good. I can really see you as Kate. How come you didn't try out?"

I hesitated, not sure how much I should say. "I've

always thought of myself as a behind-the-scenes person. I guess it just never occurred to me to read for a part."

He leaned over and kissed me lightly. "They say there should be some chemistry between the leading man and leading lady. Let's see how that works."

I caught my breath and looked into his grey eyes. "Did you try for chemistry with Lisa?"

He laughed and took my hand. "I'll never tell."

Dress rehearsal was the next day and it was a disaster. Part way through the first act as she was making an entrance, Lisa collapsed and we couldn't get bring her to. Melissa was on her hands and knees patting Lisa's face and putting tissues soaked in cold water on her forehead, but nothing worked. Lisa's breathing was shallow and her stage makeup made her look ghostly.

Melissa told me to call for an ambulance and then rode with her to the hospital. The rest of us sat at the theatre and waited for news. The mood was pretty sombre. Nobody said much. Mostly we just sat and waited and worried.

After a while, Melissa called. The doctors didn't know yet what was wrong with Lisa. A whole battery of tests had been ordered. Meanwhile, Melissa wanted us to go on with the rehearsal and for me to play Kate. It was a pretty sure bet that Lisa wouldn't be able to open the next night. I told Bill to take over in the projection booth, and moved into place on stage. That secret rehearsing with Darren paid off. We were able to carry off the dress rehearsal with surprisingly few difficulties.

I was awakened early the next morning from a pleasant dream about Darren by the ringing of the telephone. It was Melissa.

"Can you meet me at the coffee shop in an hour?"

She was waiting for me when I arrived. A cup of

coffee was already on the table in front of me. "How did the dress go last night?"

"Not too badly. I think we'll be okay for tonight. I know how much you have riding on this, Mel. Everyone's gonna do their best. Any word on Lisa? I didn't know whether I should call her parents."

Melissa took a long sip of her coffee and stared out the window. "Best not to call. They're pretty upset. I spoke to them before I phoned you. Lisa's doctor called this morning. He said the symptoms are consistent with lead poisoning, which is pretty rare. I'm telling you this, but don't say anything to the others. I don't want anyone panicking. After all, Lisa's the only one with symptoms."

"Lead poisoning?" I frowned. "I think I read somewhere that one of the causes of the Roman Empire falling was lead poisoning. The water pipes were made out of lead and it fried their brains or something. Is there something wrong with the water system?"

"They're not sure what caused it, or if it even is lead poisoning, but yeah, they're gonna check everything, just in case."

"How's Lisa this morning?"

"Not good, but no worse than last night, so I guess that's something. Obviously she's in no shape to be on stage, so I want Bill to take over stage managing for tonight, since you have to play Kate. Can he do it on his own?"

"He took over from me last night and he was fine. He's meeting me at the theatre in an hour so that I can go through everything with him."

"Good." She nodded. " It's too late to change the programs, so we're printing an insert announcing that you're playing the part of Kate." She sighed. "Lead poisoning. Can't believe it."

"Weird."

I spent a couple of hours running through everything with Bill, then I went home and took a nap. I wanted to look and feel my best when I went on stage. I washed my hair and left early for the theatre.

The buzz of excitement was palpable. Melissa called the cast and stage crew together for a pep talk. She began by telling them that Lisa was in hospital and still undergoing tests but her condition was stable. Then she told them what they already guessed, that I would play Kate in her place. With that she told us in the time-honoured tradition of the theatre, to break a leg.

I was pumped and so was Darren. He ran his hand through my hair and told me that from now on, I was his Kurly Kate. I laughed and we agreed to meet after the show to walk home together.

The performance went well as I knew it would. Everyone tried extra hard to compensate for Lisa's absence. The audience laughed in all the right places and Bill told me he thought he saw a smile on Harley Craddock's face even from as far away as the projection booth. Melissa was ecstatic. She hugged all of us and told us we'd outdone ourselves.

I told Darren to meet me at the stage door. It would take me a while to get ready. I took my time changing out of my costume into my jeans, and cleaned my face. When I was sure I was alone, I packed up the stage makeup I'd used only on Lisa, the makeup I'd doctored with lead powder at the beginning of the season, knowing the hot overhead lights would make her skin absorb the lead and eventually poison her, opening a spot for me. I wrapped her makeup in plastic bags, and as Darren and I walked home hand-in-hand, tossed the package into a dumpster.

"What's that?" He asked.

"Just some garbage," I said and smiled up at him. Sometimes you really do have to stoop to conquer.

About Joan O' Callaghan

Joan O'Callaghan is a recipient of the *Golden Apple Award* from Queen's University Faculty of Education for Excellence in Teaching, named *Professor of the Year* by OISE/UT Students Council, as well as *Most Engaging English Instructor* and *Most Inspirational Instructor*.

She is the author of three educational books as well as two e-shorts: *George* and *For Elise*.

Visit Joan at her FaceBook Page
or Tweet with @JoanOcallaghan

INCOMPETENCE KILLS

M.H. Callway

Competence is a commodity in low supply. Amazing that the world functions at all really. But incompetence does have an upside: it creates such temping opportunities for predators.

Like me.

You'd never give me a second glance. In appearance, I'm pale and bland. The only remarkable thing about me is a black spot under my thumbnail. If you bothered to get to know me better, you'd recognize it as a sign of my true nature.

Inconspicuous and invidious.

How trusting you people are. The coffee cup unattended in the food court, the step too close to the subway platform...

Innocent and inattentive.

Lucky for you that I've learned to, shall we say, engineer my violent tendencies.

Take Miranda, for instance, chattering on her phone all day long in the cubicle next to mine. Hardly a conversation, I call it "monversation": a non-stop stream of complaints about her miserable lack of challenge at work. Well, perhaps if she actually did some work for a change...

Indolent and incompetent.

So this morning I gave her the challenge she so fervently desired. I hacked into her computer system and slid a dollop of company cash into her personal bank account. The amount? Perfectly equal to her frightening lawyer's fees, a figure helpfully supplied through the echo-chamber of her office.

Indiscreet and incompetent.

Shock and awe as security marches her off the premises. I rub my black spot, savouring the blissful quiet now that she's gone. And, I want you to take note, no violence necessary.

I soldier on, in blind service to the company, the brave widow in tech support. You see, I'm mourning my dear, departed Barry, once the head of software engineering. Our marriage lasted only a year, how sad. Especially after the hard work to pry him loose from Miranda.

I rub my black spot.

Barry and Miranda, two dullards joined together in a live-in arrangement of convenience. Yes, Barry's paid-off house and his investment portfolio, plumped up by thrift and a boring life, proved convenient indeed.

For me.

Boring and bland on the outside, red fire on the inside. Barry and I were more alike than he ever knew. Quite the challenge to crack his security codes so I could ferret out his favorite kinky websites and become his fantasy woman.

Even if I had to hold my nose to do it.

Intemperate and invidious.

And so we were married. Such a shame Barry insisted on clinging to his old tight-fisted ways. He just didn't believe in the joint ownership of *anything*. Alas, he'd had his own way for far too long, first as an only child indulged by his parents, then pampered for years by Miranda, that doormat.

Intransigent and imprudent.

Barry brought it on himself. You do see that, don't you? I really do try to avoid violence whenever possible. To be honest, I do find it thrilling, but the risk...

Did I mention that I graduated as a biomedical engineer? During one of our more exotic evenings, where I played nurse and Barry became the naughty patient, I injected him with a full vial of insulin, not saline solution as he supposed.

Inconspicuous and inevitable.

My cell phone rings, startling me. Barry's lawyer must see me without delay. I feel an unfamiliar flutter of panic. Barry's will was straightforward, I assure myself. All goes to me. I made sure of that.

But when I arrive at the lawyer's office, she looks distressed. She sits me down.

Turns out Barry stayed as true to his nature as I have to mine. Ten years ago, to protect his money from Miranda, he made her sign a co-habitation agreement. Miranda, that sly bitch, is suing for her share of the spoils.

Impossible and inconceivable.

How could I slip up? I scrutinized every document Barry kept in the house after we were married. Not a hint about that old agreement sleeping in his lawyer's vault. Barry and the lawyer assumed our marriage rendered it invalid. Both were mistaken.

Incompetence!

The lawyer advises me to settle. Miranda's lawyer is expert, her case impregnable. If I fight, the legal fees will devour my share.

I rise to leave but there is more bad news. The lawyer begs my forgiveness. Miranda, pudgy, hopeless Miranda, has a new fiancé – a police officer. She has made wild accusations about Barry's sad and untimely death. The police will be asking questions. Until all is resolved, Barry's assets remain frozen.

I shed a few tears, let the lawyer pat my hand and leave.

Alone in the elevator, I rub my black spot, ready for battle. No need to worry: I had Barry cremated – and quickly, too. But should the police examine my life too closely...

And I want that money. I worked hard for it. It's mine.

Obviously Miranda deserves a violent solution, but the risk is high. I must be wonderfully subtle and effective.

Invisible and inescapable.

Why on earth is my cell phone ringing again? I go to turn it off - I've had enough of that idiot lawyer – but it isn't her, it's my doctor. He must see me immediately.

Now what?

I drop by the doctor's office. He sits me down, begs my forgiveness. He should have taken more care.

On my last visit, his young intern insisted on testing my black spot. It may be my talisman, but it's also melanoma. The tests say it has spread.

Incurable and inevitable.

How apt, you say, the universe has rebalanced. Erased a predator from civilized society. But that's not it at all, sweet heart. The universe really doesn't care about your nice little world.

It was simply incompetence. Truly, it will be the death of me.

About M.H. (Madeleine) Callway

Madeleine's stories have been published by several magazines and anthologies. This year, her story, *The Lizard,* won the Bony Pete prize sponsored by Bloody Words, Canada's national crime writers conference. Her debut novel, *Gunning for Bear,* was short-listed for the 2012 Unhanged Arthur award and previously for the Debut Dagger award. It is now under review by a major publisher of Canadian crime fiction.

Visit Madeleine at her Website
http://www.mhcallway.com/
or at her FaceBook page

FAMILY VALUES

Sylvia Maultash Warsh

He was an eighty-year-old horror, thought Libby, stirring the tomato sauce on the stovetop.

Still lived in that ancient house, a wretched old man who hated everyone. *He* should have been the one to lose his memory and forget their only child. Not Mama, who loved her. Who always took her side and protected her from his rages. Who lately peered at her, trying to excavate some memory of her daughter from an unyielding mind.

Mama's old age pension barely covered the bed in the short-staffed nursing home. She shared a cramped room with three other crazy women, one who screamed day and night. Libby had asked about the price of a private room. Well beyond her office administrator's salary, it turned out. And how long would that job last, now that she had let herself go, hair unkempt, clothes haphazard?

She carefully steamed the cabbage leaves in the pot. The home said her mother was agitated all day until Libby arrived after work. No wonder. By the time she got there, Mama's diaper was soiled and she was starving. Libby was exhausted, going daily. Her father never visited. The home suggested she pay a caregiver to be with Mama while she was at work. But that took money.

The house would bring in money. Yet her father would never agree to sell. And he could be around for another twenty years, still tall and strong for eighty. Anger kept him going. While she was at home he had slapped her regularly. She was a pile of crap, he said. Why couldn't he have a son?

She hadn't spoken to him in months. The last time she phoned, he cursed her and hung up. Maybe she could convince him to sell. Fat chance. But he did have a soft spot.

One evening she arrived at his door carrying a warm foil-covered pan.

"Get the hell outa here!" he yelled behind the closed door.

"I brought you something. Cabbage rolls." He hated to cook, loathed meals-on-wheels. Cabbage rolls were his favourite.

He opened the door, squinting at her with disgust. "How do I know you didn't poison them?"

"I'll have some too."

He let her in. He looked thinner, a bit stooped. Still a head taller than her, a force to be reckoned with.

In the kitchen she served the rolls. He sat down and started to eat, ignoring her.

"I want to sell the house," she said.

He stopped chewing. "Did your mother send you?"

"Yes, she wants you to sell." Libby avoided his eyes.

"She was always a crazy bitch. Tell her to go to hell!" He pointed at her plate. "You're not eating."

She took a bite to reassure him. He resumed eating.

She rose quietly as if going to the counter. Instead, she stopped behind him. He would never change. Just grow meaner with age. Crueler. She took the clear plastic bag from her pocket. Holding her breath, she flung the bag over his head and pressed it against his face.

He screamed, outraged, clawing at the bag. He was half-choking, half-coughing. She held the bag tight, hardened by the memory of his hand on her face, the burden of his insults.

Unexpectedly, he swung his elbow back and jabbed her in the stomach. The pain almost made her let go of the bag. But she thought of her darling mother and held on, till the plastic filled all the crevices of his face.

About Sylvia Maultash Warsh

Sylvia Maultash Warsh writes the award-winning *Dr. Rebecca Temple mystery series*. Her historical novel, *The Queen of Unforgetting*, published in 2010, was chosen for a plaque by Project Bookmark Canada. *Best Girl*, a Rapid Reads book, came out in 2012. She lives in Toronto where she teaches writing to seniors.

Visit Sylvia at her Website
http://www.sylviawarsh.com/
or look for her books at Amazon dot ca

GIVING THANKS

Kathleen Bjorn

Cara Robinson wakes to begin the preparation of the Thanksgiving dinner. She pays no mind to the tear-stained pillow.

Bill, her husband, is nowhere to be found. The same holds true for her seventeen-year-old daughter Casey, fourteen-year-old son David, and here twelve-year-old son Chris. Bill has probably taken the kids outside to play football and Frisbee. She can hear the faint songs of play outside the window. The day is clear and unseasonably warm. Perfect for play —and every Thanksgiving they play, she toils.

The pumpkin pies are still sitting on their cooling racks and the pie smell still permeates the air as she descends the stairs to the kitchen. She sees that a small wedge has been removed from one of the pies. Bill never can wait for his pumpkin pie. It is the perfect breakfast food he says every Thanksgiving. (Is that the phone? No.)

The fourteen-pound turkey is stuffed and ready to be placed into the oven right on time. With the oven door open she carefully lifts the roasting pan and slides the turkey into the chamber. (Is that the phone? No.)

She ascends the stairs to take a shower and get dressed for dinner. Bill and the kids don't believe in all the pomp and circumstance of dressing up for dinner. They would sit around the table with the outdoor smells and the incidental remnants of play on their clothes. (Is that the phone? No.)

This is Bill's favorite dress. Casey loves these shoes. David has some weird affection for the scarf. And for Chris she wears Victoria, a cologne he says smells like her so it is his favorite. She is careful to spray a mere hug scent, not one that will overpower the smells of Thanksgiving. (Is that the phone? No.)

Carefully placing the last .995 sterling dinner fork next to her grandmother's china she calls for Casey to bring the cranberry sauce to the table. No answer from Casey but is that the phone ringing? No.

She yells out the front door for the family to come in and get washed up for dinner. There comes no answer but she does notice that the play songs suddenly cease. (Is that the phone? No.)

Now she's carrying the fourteen-pound stuffed bird to the table. The yams have their place in front of David's setting, the corn, its place in front of Chris. The cranberry sauce sits in front of Casey. The gravy sits in front of her own plate. The turkey, the crown of the Thanksgiving coronation, is set in front of Bill's plate. He will carve it. (Is that the phone? Yes.)

She runs to the kitchen to answer the phone, yelling that dinner is on the table. The phone is no longer ringing but she lifts the receiver to her ear. It's a recording, a recording made four years ago this Thanksgiving Day.

"Mrs. Robinson, my name is Matt Stone, I know you don't know me but I found your number here. There's been a terrible accident and I think they might all be dead. The police and ambulance have been called but no one has answered yet. I'm so sorry to have called but I thought you should know." The phone goes dead.

She again ascends the stairs, carefully removes her Casey-loved shoes and places them in their box. She unties and removes her David-loved scarf, folds it and places it in the third drawer, the scented one, of her bureau. Her Bill-loved dress slides down around her ankles. She steps out of the dress and carefully hangs it on the satin padded hanger. Her scent, her Chris-loved mommy smell is all that remains. It will stay there so that he can find his way back to her when he needs comforting.

Her pillow beckons...the tears again, as the dinner grows cold.

Visit Kathleen Bjoran at her Website
or at her FaceBook Page

THE BATTLE OF BEAVERCOAT

Melodie Campbell

Canadian Authors' Association pick
First Published in The Hamilton Spectator

Mary trundled up the broken sidewalk, feeling very much her sixty-eight years.

These young doctors…"stout," he had called her! And she, only 160 pounds (well, 180 on the doctor's scales, but everyone knew there was something wrong with them.) In old Doctor Briscoe's day, they would have said "healthy." Instead, today, this one said lose twenty pounds.

"Cut out butter and sweets for a start. You're not getting any younger, you know. Time to watch out for cholesterol and diabetes."

It was all too miserable. And here she had been so looking forward to her afternoon tea with cookies and tarts. She deserved it too, after such a tiring day. Maybe if she did without two lumps of sugar in her tea…

Mary walked wearily, defeated by the November wind and the doctor's icy voice. The five wooden steps to her from door seemed suddenly higher and formidable. The house was old…older than she was. A distant relative had built it before the American war. It had seen the turn of two centuries and it was past its prime. The roofline sagged on two sides and the stone foundation was crumbling. Yet it was a good house, stoic and proud. Still ready to do its duty. Not ready to say goodbye.

Mary dragged each sensibly clad foot up one step at a time, waiting for the right foot to meet its mate before lifting the left one still higher. At the top of the landing she reached for the screen door, balanced it against her back, opened her vinyl organizer bag and struggled to locate keys.

Ten years ago, Len would have unlocked the front door while she stood patiently by, waiting for it, and the screen to be held open for her. But those days were gone and so was Len. Mary opened her own doors now. Sometimes they seemed uncommonly heavy.

Not today, thought. Today, the door swung inward before she had the key in the lock.

"Hello?" Surely not. She couldn't have. She pushed the door further in and poked her head around the corner. Muddy tracks led from the welcome mat, down the hall to the back kitchen.

"Hello, is anyone there?" Mary shuffled cautiously in the vestibule, clutching her purse in front of her. For a brief moment, she wondered if she had stepped through the looking glass instead. The hallway was suddenly a bewildering place. Remnants of a particularly violent tea party littered the floor. Two sterling silver teaspoons and a broken teacup lay across the entry to the parlor. A china rabbit had mysteriously leaped from her collection in the front window to commit suicide on the second stair. Somewhere, drawers were opening and closing of their own accord. Upstairs, it sounds like the Mad Hatter was jumping on the bed.

A flurry of activity in the next room left her blinking away Cheshire cats and staring at an all too human male.

"What are you doing?" she squeaked. A young man streaked by her, barely a blur in the hallway, grabbed the handbag from her trembling fingers, and bounded out of the house. Mary fell back against the wall, faint with confusion.

"Help!" It came out a feeble bird-chirp. Oh, this was dreadful! Her purse gone! Robbers everywhere, stealing her things. Where was Sergeant Thompkin? Who would help? She shuddered and tried to focus on producing a really good scream.

Another man was running down the stairs, two at a time, with something bulky in his arms, brown and bulging. Mary stared at the familiar bundle bouncing toward her most unnaturally.

Her beaver coat! Hers! Dark brown sheared beaver, for which she had scrimped and saved for years and years, working at the bank…only to find out later from her niece in biophysics that it wasn't politically correct or even nice to wear dead animal skins - only now they say it is all right again, because fur is a renewable resource and supports the native culture – and now this skinny boy, this *punk*, with greasy hair and bloodshot eyes and who know what venereal diseases was going to run out the door with her coat…This was too much.

"Not my beaver!" She screamed and launched herself at the intruder.

The boy yelped and tried to shield his face from the clawing hands. But he was no match for her. Oh no – a skinny kid from the street was no match for someone whose ancestors had come over on the Mayflower. Well, maybe not the Mayflower exactly, but soon after it, and they had fought the Indians! Pioneers, they were, not to mention United Empire Loyalists, and the Boer War, the United Church and Baden Powell and the whole Girl Guide movement, which she herself had been involved with all her long life.

Hah! No mere punk of a boy could expect to deal with *that*. With an animal scream she wrenched the massive coat out of his arms and stumbled back against the wall. Indian yells continued to screech from behind a flailing curtain of soft brown fur.

The wooden screen door banged shut. Running feet echoed on the wooden steps, hit the grass, and faded abruptly.

Back in the front hall, Mary sat in a heap, hugging the beaver coat with all her might.

"Well," she said, pushing herself up from the plank floor. Her tweed skirt had ridden up rather badly. She smoothed it down with one hand. Next, she held up the coat to check for damage. One rip across the top of the shoulder continued down the length of the armhole. Nothing that couldn't be mended. She clucked with satisfaction.

Then Mary did what any good woman whose ancestors had come over on the Mayflower – or at least shortly after it – would do. She put on her beaver coat, first one arm, then the next, and – with battle-worn torn shoulder flapping like a flag in the breeze – marched briskly down to police headquarters to report the break-in to Sergeant Thompkin.

About Melodie Campbell

Melodie Campbell got her start writing comedy. In 1999, she opened the Canadian Humour Conference. Her third novel, *The Goddaughter*, is a comic mob caper. Melodie was a finalist for both the 2012 Derringer and Arthur Ellis Awards, and is the Executive Director of Crime Writers of Canada.

Visit Melodie at her Website
http://www.melodiecampbell.com/
or at her FunnyGirlMelodie BlogSpot

TREASURES IN THE ATTIC

A.C. Cargill

Climbing up the creaky stairs,
She slowly enters attic space.
Darkness reigns o'er musty airs
Gives solemn visage to this place.

Oaken beams with cobwebs hold
Roof above this treasure mine,
Boxes piled up, dust so old
Thick on cardboard without line.

Pulling chain, the bulb she lights,
Blinks a time or two to see
Labeled boxes, welcome sights,
Special contents, mystery.

Pandora did open box,
Spread on world a plague of pain,
Sent by Zeus to punish man
For a trick of off'ring lain.

Treasure hunters dig in sand,
Foll'wing map so quickly drawn
On the shore of native land,
Find the chest at rise of dawn.

Does a carton hold such ills
From a creature bent on harm?

Or some memories' small thrills
Like a treasure full of charm?

In a corner cast in shade
Stands victrola under sheet.
Handle crank and sound is made,
Needle scratches out a beat.

Strauss' waltz in three four time
Swirls around her waiting ears,
Takes her back on music's rhyme
To those gentle ballroom years.

Dancing 'round across the plank,
Swirls she in dust like a cloud,
Stops before box, label blank,
Thinks a bit, then muses 'loud,

"What could be the treasure here?
There's no word to answer me
On the outside so austere,
So I open now to see."

With a tug inside she peeks,
Treasure hunt has just begun.
She knows not what gem she seeks,
Looks at items one by one.

First is mug all paper wrapped,
Gifted on her wedding day.
Then, a plate that's stained and cracked,
Heirloom from her Grammy May.

Deeper still she digs into
Treasures dear and so much more,
Sighs as each comes to her view,
Thinks, "Tis pleasure, not a chore."

Hair of silver gray a-shine
In the bulb's strong yellow light,
Face of aging soft skin line,
Eyes a sparkle, wise and bright,

On she goes until the end,
Fingers gently each enfold
Like an old and dearest friend
Full of stories yet untold.

Calls her husband up the stairs,
"Are you done with hunting, dear?
Kettle's whistled, tea brew airs
Fill the kitchen, strong and clear."

"Coming," she calls, "with my prize."
Waltz is done, victrola still,
Record back into sleeve lies.
Down the stairs she steps with thrill.

Into waiting arms she glides,
Old-time true love to embrace,
Shows him treasure in hand rides,
Long-forgotten crystal vase.

To the kitchen where tea brews
They both stroll with smiling face,
Pour their tea and spice cake choose,
Put a rose in that old vase.

"Single rose for you, my wife,"
He croons softly in her ear.
"Ah," she says, "you are my life,"
Sniffs the rose and hugs him near.

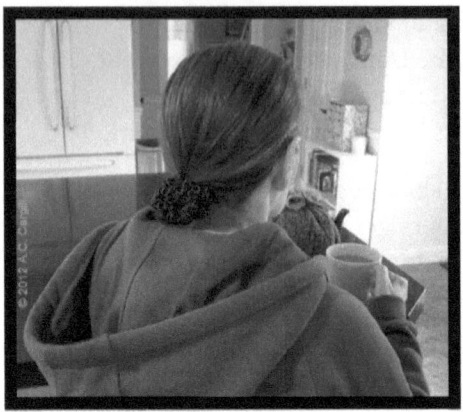

About A.C. Cargill

A.C. Cargill blogs about tea, writes poetry about tea, drinks tea, and enjoys time with her hubby who also drinks tea. She has written a variety of items, including user guides and marketing materials, and finally decided to do some writing that was a bit more fun. Thus the poetry!

Visit A.C. at her Website: Tea Time with A.C. Cargill
http://www.teatimewithaccargill.blogspot.ca/
or on FaceBook

DANCE

Rosalind Croucher

No one would wear a party hat
and dance with me.
I was the only fool who would admit it.
Celebrate it.
Saw the fools we are
when we half-smile
and pretend control.
In this life
These musical chairs
No one to spin and flail with me.
Even just
for this one dance.

About Rosalind Croucher

Rosalind Croucher went to school some places, worked some places and wrote some stuff. Lists mostly. Loves writing a good list. She is currently compiling, charting, cross-referencing, graphing and tabulating a list of books she'd like to write. It's very pretty. She currently lives and works in Toronto.

Visit Rosalind at FaceBook
or Tweet with her @RMCroucher

FINDING CALM

Sheila Jeffries

Storm squeaks inside me like a corkscrew,
vortex crying to vortex
through the seas.

She is huge and sweeping trouble,
twisting the pines like tea towels
until they creak.

The colour of thunder in my heart
has guilty silhouettes
of needs.

The crumbling of the light, an accusation,
embosses my footsteps
on the leaves.

I feel the folded oak bud sleeping,
the twig's vibration and the stippled shouts
of trees

cry storm and crazy-crack the sky,
swap spirals, pirouette
and meet.

Our hair flares out for miles across the sun,
beaded with hailstones, burrs
and thistle seeds.

We snake together, storm and I,
she sucks the anger from my bones.
My eyes search deep,

find calm in her heart, in a crack
of the cork oak's bark, the red
of a ladybird asleep.

About Sheila Jeffries

Sheila Jeffries is the author of twelve children's books under the names Sheila Haigh and Sheila Chapman. Now writing as Sheila Jeffries, she has just published *SOLOMON'S TALE*, and is working on an adult three book saga. She lives in Somerset UK.

Visit Sheila at her Website:
http://www.sheilajeffries.com/
or at her Amazon Author Page

MURMUR

Mike Slater

Who said we knew
Or thought about it even?
Should one suggest
Our mind perfect pure reason?

Is that the sport
A parlance of the vulgar?
Nothing to cure
The curse that we are under?

Should we prevail
Supplant despair, our Sister?
And draw pure air
Behold our own elixir?

A million souls
Lost searching for the latter
Religious thoughts
Collide and veil pure matter

But nature speaks
The sun and stars do murmur
Though one not hear
The Truth still travels further

About Michael C. Slater

Michael C. Slater loves words. It all started in grade school with vocabulary tests. Sometimes, it was augmented by having to copy the dictionary when 'in trouble' and even more words were learned. Currently, Michael tries to capture emotions he sees on display with words instead of a camera.

Visit Michael at FaceBook
or Tweet with him @MikeCSlater

FOSTERING HUMANITY MANIFESTO

Paulissa Kipp

Leonard Cohen observes that "everything has a crack, that's how the light gets in".

We soak up the rays, tell time and mark the seasons with the sun and grow with the help of the sun. We turn our faces to the sun, always seeking the good, the beautiful and the happiness we believe is found there.

Yet the pursuit of happiness and warmth of the sun often causes those who are the most vulnerable to be overlooked. Darkness brings fear, anxiety, monsters under the bed and cold truths we might rather avoid. It is easy to see the light, yet darkness has value as well. There we find the lost and lonely who are always left behind. The homeless, the veteran, the mentally disabled, those with depression or any one of us on a given day who need a kind word, a gentle touch, a smile and understanding.

Instead, many of us look away as though by not laying eyes on humanity and need, it will not exist. Yet vulnerability and the need for love always exists and neither ignorance nor apathy will change that. The only thing that changes darkness and neglect is love. You don't have to love someone romantically to practice love. The challenge is this: Do not cause harm. Give the benefit of the doubt. We do not inhabit another's mind so we will never know the full story at any given time. Simple recognition of that fact will go a long way toward fostering humanity.

I have been asked many times what fostering humanity means so I will attempt to share my vision here:

> 1- <u>No one</u> is insignificant. Never brush aside anyone as insignificant. Who knows what they can teach us?

> 2- "Treat the other man's faith gently; it is all he has to believe with. His mind was created for his own thoughts, not yours or mine." ~ Henry S. Haskins

> Whether a person is a believer in a higher power or not, do not tear at the fabric of another's belief system to feed your ego. We all come to faith (by that I do not necessarily mean religion) in our own ways and our own time. Who is to say that the person who walks silently along a brook doesn't feel moved by a spirit? Allow each person to engage in his or her own belief system. At the end of the day, it matters most whether or not a person is kind.

> 3- Choose love. It is easy to be negative, to think that others have it in for us and to think the worst.

> 4- Protect the vulnerable. Don't assume that someone else will be your backbone.

> 5- Listen to others. The most basic human need is someone to tell our story to. It matters.

6- Make your points without personal attacks. Weak people attack others instead of clearly and civilly stating disagreements and trying to find common ground. When common ground can't be found, wish your "opponent" well.

7- Find beauty in everyone. Everyone has it. If it isn't apparent, that means that you haven't waited long enough. Everyone has humanity to be laid thread by golden thread and woven into a tapestry of joyful existence.

8- Add joy where you can. Kindness costs nothing.

9- Label no one. Labels negate worth.

We are all magnificent; we are all capable of love, hope, kindness and beauty manifested. You have more to offer than you could ever imagine and the universe is waiting.

I leave you with this:

Let me assure you that you are loved. You were wonderfully created, and made to be someone special. You are ever changing but in every phase you are a perfect master piece. You are beautiful, you are wonderful, and you cannot fail. You were not made for that. You were made to be a beautiful human becoming, not a beggar. You were made to be a warrior, not a doormat. YOU ARE A WARRIOR! Stand tall. Know that you are more than you ever imagined. Know you are worthy of every blessing. Know you are loved more than you ever imagined.

Foster Humanity.

About Paulissa Kipp

Paulissa Kipp uses her experience as an observer of life to document her world - the beautiful, the curious and the overlooked. Her works have been featured in THE JOURNEY: WOMEN'S WRITING FROM THE HEART, THE PLUSONE COLLECTION, HOW WE SEE IT and numerous other publications.

Visit Paulissa at her Website
www.redbubble.com/people/paulissaism/portfolio
or at her Google + Page

COLE'S NOTES

Melanie Robertson-King

Cole pulled the heavy, oak door closed behind him.

Pausing, he looked up at the low hanging, gunmetal grey clouds gathering over the Castlegate. A storm was imminent. An icy blast of wind sent the dried autumn leaves on the sidewalk swirling into the air. It wasn't yet the middle of October but the weather had been unseasonably cold this fall. The hot, dry summer was now a fading memory.

He blew into his hands to warm them before putting the hood up on the fleece he wore under his worn, brown leather bomber jacket, and zipped his coat up. Afterwards, he shoved his hands into his front jeans pockets and jogged down the steps.

The damp wind from the North Sea hit him like he had walked into a granite wall, when Cole turned onto Union Street from Bon Accord Crescent. The tall buildings concentrated the gale, making it hard for him to walk. The air felt and smelled of rain and he hoped it would hold off until he reached Starbucks. In an effort to beat the rapidly approaching inclement weather, Cole quickened his pace.

A few steps short of his destination, the skies opened and the deluge began. When he reached the sheltered entranceway, Cole yanked his wet hood down and shook his jacket, sending out a spray of water droplets.

Joining the queue lined up in front of the counter, he shifted nervously while he waited his turn. Sweat gathered around his collar and it wasn't just because it was warm inside the coffee shop. The narrow corridor created by shelving units holding bags of coffee—ground and beans, mugs and travel cups, made him feel claustrophobic. At least the stools by the window were still available. He always sat there—the same seat every day—the one at the end on the right. He hoped the people ahead of him wouldn't take them.

"First, please," the clerk called out.

Initially, he didn't realize she meant him. He shuffled to the counter.

"Your usual, Cole?" she asked.

He nodded and looked down at his scruffy shoes. Jeannie was pretty and friendly and sometimes if she had a moment when she wiped off the counter at the window where he always sat, she spoke to him. He liked her but was painfully shy and didn't have the bottle to say much in response, other than please, thank you and keep the change.

"You go get your place by the window and I'll bring it over."

Cole looked over his shoulder. Jeannie was right. Only one seat left in front of the window—his favorite one. "Th-thank you," he mumbled as he walked away.

A few minutes later, Jeannie placed his steaming hot latte was in front of him. "Enjoy it, Cole," she said, smiling.

Her big blue eyes sparkled like the sun on the North Sea. Her teeth were perfectly straight and white and she had a flawless complexion save for a single dark mole high on her cheekbone about an inch under her right eye. Cole thought it gave her an added air of mystery and glamour. He had heard her complain to co-workers and female customers about having it removed. He couldn't bear it if she did. It was a part of her, something that made her unique. Her brown hair was long, but how long he didn't know because she always pulled it back in a pony tail. If only he could work up the nerve to ask her out on a date, maybe she would wear it down. Cole tried to imagine what it would look like falling softly around her face and possibly past her shoulders. "Thank you," he finally mumbled.

After Jeannie had left him to his latte, Cole pulled his grotty, black leather covered notebook out of his inside breast pocket and opened it to the page marked by a shabby, blue ribbon. He stared out onto the street and watched the people walk past—some with umbrellas, others sheltering under their briefcases or newspapers.

Next, Cole pulled out his Bic pens, red, black and blue, and lined them up evenly on the counter. He stared at them before finally choosing the blue one. Taking the cap off, he stuck it on the plug end and chewed on it momentarily before putting pen to paper. Soon the ink flowed. He worked furiously pausing briefly to sip his latte.

"What are you writing?" Jeannie asked while she cleared away plates, mugs, and napkins from the vacancies left from where customers had sat along the counter.

Cole slammed his notebook closed. No one could see what he'd been working on. That notebook was his personal property. Only he could read the words on those pages. "N-nothing," he replied.

"You can tell me," she said as she slid onto the stool next to him. "I won't tell anyone."

"No!" Cole exclaimed as he put the cap back on his pen and stuffed his belongings inside his jacket before he pushed his way past her and out the door.

***

It had been over a week since Cole had come in, making Jeannie worry. It was so out of character. She hoped he had gone off to visit family elsewhere, or worst case scenario was stuck in at home with a cold or the flu.

Every time the door opened, she looked up expectantly hoping to see him in the entranceway and every time she was disappointed.

After closing one night when they were cleaning up, her co-worker, Rick, discovered something. "Jeannie, come here," he called.

"What is it?"

"Doesn't this belong to your 'boyfriend', Cole?" he held a notebook up in his hands. The pages were beginning to fall out.

"Give me that!" Jeannie reached out to grab it.

Rick lifted it higher. "He was a weirdo, you should know that more than the rest of us," he taunted, waving the book in front of her just out of her reach.

"Give me that," she yelled again and lunged at him. Dislodging the notebook, Jeannie scrambled for it the minute it hit the floor. "Now back off. What's written in here is none of anyone's business. I'll drop it by Cole's flat on my way home," she said as she shoved the loose pages back inside it.

"And just how do you know where he lives?" he mocked.

"I'll find out," she snapped, stuffing the notebook into her apron pocket.

***

Later that afternoon while on break, Jeannie pulled the leather covered object out and turned it over carefully in her hands. The last time she'd seen Cole was the day he'd rushed out of the coffee shop panicked. That was the day she had asked him what he had been writing. But how did his notebook end up on the floor? She'd watched him put it in his pocket. It didn't slip out that she recalled. She would have seen it or heard it hit the floor. And if that was the case, she would have chased after him right then to return it.

Jeannie wanted to open it and read the contents but as she told Rick, it was personal. But what harm would there be in just taking a look on the inside front cover or maybe even the flyleaf? With any luck, the information she needed to return it would be written there. She wouldn't look any place else. If she was lucky enough to find his address, she would return the notebook at the end of her shift. If not, she would keep it in her large handbag until she saw Cole again.

After much deliberation, Jeannie opened the front cover. There was nothing to identify him. But there was a pen and ink sketch he'd done of her—hair down—and descriptive words about her surrounding it. Jeannie—kind, pretty, friendly were just a few of the words that registered. Now intrigued, she turned the page. She recognized some of the sketches as people who frequented the coffee shop and snickered at the words Cole had chosen to for them.

Rick was in there, too. She couldn't suppress her laughter at what Cole thought of him. The adjectives she liked best were pompous and arsewipe.

She turned one more page and immediately wished she hadn't. The sketch here wasn't a person Jeannie recognized but he'd labeled it 'Mother'. The words surrounding it weren't what she expected to read when referring to the woman who brought you into the world... 'bitch, dark places, locked up, men, hooker, slut, hate you.'

Curiosity aroused by what she'd seen on the pages before her, Jeannie wanted to continue. She'd promised herself she'd only look for his name and address so she could return it to him and she'd done that albeit unsuccessfully.

"Thought you weren't going to look in it?" Rick sneered.

Slamming the notebook shut, Jeannie shoved it back into her apron pocket. "Only looking for his address. I was hoping he would have written it down near the front."

At the end of her shift, she placed the notebook in her large handbag and went home to her flat. When she opened the door, Murphy, her ginger and white cat hissed and swatted at her leg when she hit him.

She dropped her handbag onto her small dinette table and walked to the kitchen, opened her fridge and peered in. An open bottle of Riesling stood in the lower shelf in the door. She pulled it out by the neck and shut the door with her hip as she turned to get a glass from the rack affixed to the bottom of her upper cabinets.

Sitting at the table, Jeannie poured the wine and took a sip. She worried about Cole. He was always so predictable you could set your watch by him. Every day, the same time, the same latte, the same stool by the window. Yes, he was a bit odd but there had been customers come into Starbucks who were far stranger than he.

Jeannie pulled the notebook out of her handbag and placed it on the table in front of her. She rubbed the cover lightly with the palm of her hand. In places it was worn so thin, the paper backing on the inside almost visible. She opened it to the page marked by the ribbon. It was another sketch of her but without her mole. She reached up instinctively and touched her face then looked back at the page. Cole had written 'must keep mole, glamorous, pretty, not Jeannie without it' around the picture. Until then, she didn't know he felt so strongly about the possibility of her having it removed, let alone him having an opinion of any kind about it. Suddenly, she felt frightened. Was Cole some kind of control freak? Would he hurt her if she went ahead with the surgery to remove it?

Feeling dirty and cheap, Jeannie slammed the notebook shut and pushed it away. She took the bottle of wine and her glass, ensured the flat door was locked and the chain on and headed for the bathroom, locking that door behind her, too. Soon the tub was filling with hot, steamy water. She poured a few drops of Green Apple bath and shower gel in. A sea of bubbles formed and floated on the rising water. Jeannie flipped the switch on her heated towel bar.

Before the tub filled completely, she moved her caddy from the opposite end towards the taps, topped up her wine glass and placed it in the specially designed holder, stripped and climbed in. She turned the water off and slowly sank below the bubbles.

Luxuriating in the hot, soapy water Jeannie let her mind wander. Perhaps she was making too much of the mole on her face. It wasn't huge. It hadn't changed. It was flat and dark and been there for as long as she could remember. She'd not made an appointment to have it removed. Maybe she wouldn't.

Her thoughts returned to the page in Cole's notebook where he had described his mother in such an unflattering way. She took a sip of wine then sank back under the water wishing she'd turned the heat up in the room before getting into the bath.

When pounding on her flat door startled her, Jeannie leapt out of the water, almost knocking the caddy and wine flying. She didn't take the time to grab one of her warmed towels, just pulled on her long, pink, fleece dressing gown. She was still struggling with the tie belt when she reached the door.

Her cordless phone was in the base so she grabbed the handset before she looked through the peephole. It was Rick. What was he doing at her flat at this time of night? She opened the door a crack but left the chain firmly on the latch. "What's going on?"

"Can we come in? It's important."

"We?"

"Yes. Let's not stand here all night debating this," he replied impatiently.

Jeannie removed the chain and opened the door to receive Rick and whoever was with him.

"This is Dr Baird. She's Cole's shrink."

"Psychiatrist," the well-groomed woman corrected.

"Wh-why are you here?" Jeannie stammered.

"Can we sit down?" the doctor asked.

"Yes," Jeannie escorted them to the table. She picked Cole's notebook up and shoved it into her large handbag and tossed it onto the peninsula counter before showing them each a chair.

"I came in to coffee shop looking for you," Dr Baird said as she nodded at Jeannie. "Cole missed his last two appointments which isn't like him. One I could see due to illness but not both."

"Wh-what does that have to do with me?"

"He always spoke of you during our sessions. He thought you were a very special young woman."

Jeannie blushed.

"You're probably wondering why I insisted your friend bring me to your flat."

"The thought has crossed my mind," Jeannie replied sarcastically.

"There's no easy way to tell you this. Cole is dead. His body was discovered in his flat earlier today. He's been dead about a week. The police contacted me when they couldn't find any next-of-kin information. My number was by his phone."

Jeannie's heart pounded so hard she thought it would explode. She stared at the psychiatrist. Her mouth gaped open. She couldn't cry. She was too stunned. About a week—that would have been right after he rushed out of Starbucks the day she asked what he'd written in his notebook. "It's all my fault," she finally wailed. "If I hadn't sat down beside him and asked what he was doing...,"

"Cole was a very disturbed young man. No one could have predicted he would do this, let alone when."

The words were of little comfort. But now the sketch in the notebook started to make sense.

"It's only in the past year that Cole has been living in his own flat. He went from the borstal where he was sent after he murdered his mother when he was twelve to a half-way house and finally when I deemed he was no longer a danger to anyone, we procured a flat for him."

Suddenly, Jeannie felt nauseous and she bolted for the bathroom, hand over her mouth. Dropping to her knees in front of the toilet and threw up again and again, retching until there was nothing left. Tears ran down her cheeks. Cole, who she thought was her friend, was a murderer. But was he really her friend? Had he been sizing her up to become his next victim?

Gradually, she picked herself up off the floor and looked in the mirror. Her mascara left dark streaks down her cheeks. Jeannie grabbed the bottle of Listerine and rinsed her mouth hoping to eliminate the bitter taste but it didn't help.

Moving robotically, she rejoined Rick and the doctor and dropped onto one of the hard dinette chairs.

Dr Baird took an envelope out of her handbag and slid it across the table to Jeannie. "He wanted you to have this if anything ever happened to him." The psychiatrist looked at Rick and said, "You'll stay here with her. She's too upset to be left alone. I'm sorry but I must go. I'll be in touch with the funeral arrangements. Don't bother getting up. I'll let myself out."

Jeannie followed the doctor's exit with her eyes. Her hand touched the envelope and she quickly recoiled.

After the psychiatrist left, Jeannie drew her knees up to her chest and planted her heels firmly on the chair, wrapped her arms around her legs and cried.

Rick tried to comfort her but he couldn't. "Let's get you into bed," he said as he helped her off the chair. He put his arm around her and walked her to her bedroom, opened the door and reached in for the light switch.

"Don't leave me, please. I don't want to be alone," she begged.

"I'm not going anywhere. I'll get a blanket and make myself comfortable on your sofa for the night."

Jeannie pointed to the closet and watched Rick open the bi-fold doors. He reached onto the shelf and pulled down a comforter. She turned her bed down and was about to untie her dressing gown when she realized she was naked under it. Instead, she climbed in with it on.

Rick stopped by her bed. "I'll turn the light out on my way to the lounge."

"No! I need you to leave it on."

He looked around the room. "Why don't I just turn a couple of these small lamps on instead? They're not as harsh and you won't be in the dark," he said as he walked around the room switching on the other lights.

She nodded. "Leave the door open, too, please."

He nodded, switched the ceiling light off and went into the other room.

For hours, Jeannie lay and stared at the ceiling. She

couldn't believe what she'd been told about Cole. Dr Baird hadn't said he'd killed himself but it sounded like he had. But why? What had she done that day in Starbucks to drive him to it? Surely wanting to see inside his notebook wasn't that extreme? Eventually, she fell into a restless sleep.

The next morning, Jeannie was up before the sun rose. Rick remained on the sofa, snoring in ignorant bliss of the torment she felt. The letter remained on the table where it had been placed the previous evening. She put the kettle on to boil and while she waited, got a mug and the instant coffee from the cupboards and the milk from the fridge. Rick groaned from the lounge. "Coffee's up if you're interested," she called out to him.

She watched him throw the comforter off. He was in his boxers and socks. She hadn't noticed his pants and shirt draped over the arm chair. She turned away so he could have a moment of privacy to get dressed.

Jeannie sat down at the table and looked at the envelope. She picked it up and examined it. The handwriting was identical to what she'd seen in Cole's notebook. The words 'To Jeannie at Starbucks... to be opened after my death' spooked her. She dropped it like it scalded her. What was so important that he couldn't tell her when he was alive?

"You not opened that yet?" Rick asked when he passed by the table on his way to make himself a coffee.

"N-no. I'm not sure I want to see what's in it."

"It's got to be something fairly important I would think. Why else would he have left you a letter?"

"I don't know. I'm not sure I want to know," she replied and laid it back on the table.

"Don't be such a wuss. Open the letter."

Jeannie picked up the envelope, walked the kitchen and tossed it into the bin. "I can't do it. I don't want to do it."

"You're making a mistake. If that letter goes out in the rubbish, you'll be kicking yourself in the arse from here to Sunday and back again."

Suddenly, she started to giggle. The words pompous and arsewipe from Cole's notebook came to mind. She couldn't look at Rick and keep a straight face.

It was a relief when he left to go to work. She had the flat to herself. She could go through her normal morning routine. She poured her cold coffee down the sink and opened the cupboard door. The bin was still there but the letter was missing. Panic set in. She wheeled around and found it on the peninsula countertop.

This letter would haunt her until she opened it. Jeannie turned it over, stuck her thumb under a loose corner of the flap tore it open. She pulled the paper out of the envelope and let the latter flutter to the floor. Carefully, she unfolded the page and began to read.

My dearest friend, Jeannie,

If you're reading this, then Dr Baird has passed my letter on to you and you'll know that I'm dead. There are many things about me that you will never understand. I don't understand some of them either.

Dr Baird has probably told you that I murdered my mother. That is true. I don't deny it. But you deserve to know why. From the time I was a little lad, she was a prostitute. Quite often, she left me alone overnight while she went out and shagged blokes for money. It wasn't to support me but her drug habit. Social services were around and every time they threatened to put me into care, she pleaded with them saying she would mend her ways and promise to be a good mum.

Her idea of being a good mum was bring her tricks back to our dingy flat. She locked me in the closet or the chest at the foot of her bed. But I knew what she was doing. I saw the men come into the bedroom, grabbing at her and her clothes. I heard them shagging. Sometimes, those blokes would beat the crap out of her and steal what earnings and drugs she had.

I know what I did was wrong. I don't think in the beginning I really meant to kill her. But after I stuck the knife in her the first time, I couldn't stop. They say I stabbed her over thirty times. Even after she was dead, I kept sticking the knife into her.

I think I did it out of some misguided loyalty. If she was dead, she was off the drugs. The blokes couldn't beat her almost to death. She'd got aids either from the dirty needles or from letting blokes do her bareback. Do you know what that means?

You were always kind to me, Jeannie. You never made fun of me. Never tried to take advantage of my weaknesses. I couldn't show you the notebook because I had drawn so many pictures of you in it. I didn't want you to think I was some sort of freak or stalker. I know some of the people you worked with did.

I would have been proud to step out with you on my arm. You're a beautiful, young woman. You must have a number of nice blokes queuing up to take you out. I would never have stood a chance.

Don't grieve for me. I've been dead inside, except when I've been in your presence, for a very long time. My topping myself was just the final act.

Remember, though, that I appreciated the kindness and friendliness you always showed me.

No matter if I'm in heaven or hell (and I don't particularly believe in either), I love you and always will. I wished I could have told you to your face.

Cole xo

***

After reading the letter he'd left for her, she'd gone through his notebook from the beginning to the last page he'd used. The sketches were amazing. He had such a talent for capturing the essence of people, not just their features.

The day of Cole's funeral came too quickly for her liking. Jeannie didn't want to go but knew she had to. She persuaded Rick to accompany her so she wouldn't have to go alone. Since the night she found out about Cole's death, Rick had been there for her.

Jeannie wore her hair down, the way Cole had sketched her more than once in his notebook. Glad that Rick came with her, she stood bravely by the graveside with the few mourners who attended. When it was over and the casket lowered, she dropped Cole's grotty, leather notebook into the grave. It landed with a resounding smack on the wooden surface of the coffin. "Goodbye, Cole. Your notes will always be private now," she murmured.

Immediately after, Jeannie dropped the long-stemmed red rose she'd brought. It landed silently beside Cole's prized possession. She whispered, "I love you, too, Cole. I wish we could have told each other our feelings."

She turned away and sobbing, buried her face in Rick's chest.

About Melanie Robertson-King

Melanie wrote non-fiction articles before she turned her love for the written word to short stories and novel-length fiction. Her first book, *A Shadow in the Past*, will be released in September 2012. A lover of Scotland and all things Scottish, she met Princess Anne on one of her trips.

Visit Melanie at her Website
http://www.melanierobertson-king.com/wp02/
or at her FaceBook Page

RUNNING PARALLEL

Tracy L. Ward

I could hear the hollow train whistle from my bedroom better than any other part of the house.

Its high tones were muted by blocks of buildings, houses and trees but the base sound rattled my skin from miles away. The rumble became a kind of lullaby to me as a child so much so that when the trains did not run on Christmas Day, everyone noticed.

"Do you hear that Lily?" My father would ask at the breakfast table, his lips almost curled around his coffee cup.

"I don't hear anything," I would answer.

"Exactly."

The tracks ran everywhere throughout town, sometimes four or five even six sets running parallel to each other before turning and merging into one. It was such a poor design for pedestrians yet exquisitely engineered for maximum haulage. The grain elevator at the end of the line on the lake shore sat as a massive reminder to all in town that our very livelihood was held in its deep hauls.

The Great Depression, as they later called it, was tightening its grip around us. Jobs were scarce, markets for our farmed goods even more so, and those that needed them could hardly afford to pay. We kids spent every day in fear of what this would mean. We heard the adults speak in hushed tone, noticed the increasing sense of unease and could tell things were different then, really different.

I was woken up early one morning, too early for a

Saturday but my brother, Charlie, cared not as he gripped my shoulders to wrestle me from my sleep. "Get up!" he demanded in a harsh whisper so no one else would hear. He was the oldest of the four of us kids, and I was the second oldest. I imagine that is why he came to me that morning instead of Jacob or Mary.

My eyes shot open when I heard his hastened voice in my ear. Gripping the quilt tightly with my fingers, I pulled it up to my chin lest my nearly grown brother see me in my nightshirt. I glanced to Mary, who as still sleeping soundly in her bed across the room, miraculously undisturbed by our brother's intrusion.

"Damn it Charlie!" I hissed back, but he ignored me.

"Get dressed and meet me in the kitchen," he said quietly and turned to leave.

I watched him leave the room, and wondered what could possibly be so important that he wake me before dawn.

I was careful to open the bureau in such a way so the wood did not squeak. I dressed quickly, but my fast movements were too loud and Mary turned in her bed. "What's going on?" she mumbled, not bothering to open her eyes.

"Nothing," I whispered, "go back to sleep."

Too tired to argue, Mary turned back into her pillow and did what she was told, a first in her lifetime.

I found Charlie in the kitchen rummaging through the cupboards pulling out a jar of jam and loaf of bread Mama had made the day before. I watched as he threw the items in a floppy flour sack and then turn back for the two tins of meat on the shelf.

"What are you doing?" I asked abandoning my whispered tone.

Instead of defending himself or offering an

explanation he flashed me a smile, the Charlie Meyer smile I could recognize anywhere. He swung the sack over his shoulder and motioned for me to follow him out the back door.

The neighborhood was completely asleep. The only movement besides ourselves were a few tom cats lounging on their owner's porches after a night on the town, waiting for their morning meal. Charlie and I walked an entire block before he said anything.

"I'm leaving," he spat out, as if the very words couldn't be held inside him any longer.

I jerked my head in his direction, challenging him with my eyes to repeat what he just said. He was barely fifteen, hardly an age to venture out on his own, especially with work for Papa so scarce. We needed him, second in command we always told him. We needed everyone. Together.

"Don't try to talk me out of it, Lily," he said turning his gaze from my own. "I met Jimmy last night and he's going to Toronto. He says his cousin has work for him there and said that I could tag along."

"Charlie you can't—"

"I will send money back when I can," he continued, "maybe enough for you and Mary to buy a new dress."

I stared at him as he walked a few paces ahead of me. I silently dared him to keep talking, knowing he was hardly making any sense. "I don't need a new dress, and neither does Mary."

I watched as he pressed his lips together but he did not waiver. He looked so determined to go and I felt it would not matter what I said.

"I asked you to come to see me off," he said.

"What about Mama, and Pa?" I asked struggling to keep up with his quickening pace.

"I didn't want a fuss, Lily!" he yelled turning to me so quickly I nearly walked right into him. "I wanted to say goodbye without Ma blubbering, and Pa threatening to tie me to the porch."

I swallowed, conceding to be silent, to do as he asked, to not make a scene.

We crossed the main street without needing to run as we normally would have to avoid the approaching automobiles. The single traffic light suspended over the intersection blinked on and off needlessly as we passed.

Jimmy was there, waiting at the side of the station smoking a cigarette, no doubt stolen from his father. Charlie's best friend was alone, apparently seeing no need to inform his family either, or perhaps he had left a hastily scribbled note on the dining room table. I suddenly imagined having to tell our mother and father, without the aid of a note. I would be solely responsible for breaking the news that their eldest son had abandoned us.

We were four or five paces from Jimmy before I grabbed Charlie's arm and pulled him back, tears streaming down my hot cheeks. "Don't do this," I said frantically.

He placed his hand on my cheek. "It's going to be okay," he said, a smile growing.

"Not getting cold feet are you?" Jimmy called out. He plucked the cigarette from his mouth and threw it to the gravel, grinding it with his foot.

Charlie shook his head. He couldn't bear to look at me. "I'm coming," he said, "Just go ahead. I won't be but a minute."

Jimmy nodded, waved his hand to me and began his march down the tracks. Once he was out of earshot Charlie turned back to me. I was a complete mess with tears streaming down my cheeks and my nose running. I wondered how he could look at me and not be convinced to stay.

"Who's gonna tell Mama?" I asked my voice laced with panic. "What's Pa going to do when you're gone? What if something happened to Pa?—"

"Ah come on! Nothing's gonna happen to Pa." Charlie seemed to laugh slightly at the suggestion.

"But what if something did? We wouldn't survive long, not with the way things are." I searched his face for any hint of hesitation. He had been so desperate to leave since we were kids and now he had a chance to go. He was leaving, boarding a freight train like some hobo and he expected me to be the one to break it to the rest of the family. "You're a coward Charlie Meyer," I spat out, suddenly disgusted with him. "A complete coward if you think you can just run off without so much as a proper goodbye."

I didn't know what to expect from him. Part of me braced for a smack in reaction to my hurtful words, the other part pleaded for just some harsh words instead. He did neither. He glanced over his shoulder to Jimmy and saw him many yards down the track.

Without a word he kissed me softly on my soggy cheek and walked away. He jogged to Jimmy's side and then kept pace as they walked the track together. I knew they planned to jump on a moving train farther down the track when no one was looking. That was the way you did it back then with no money to pay your fare. I heard a train rumbling down the farthest track, slowly since it was in town but gathering up speed as it charged along.

"A coward Charlie!" I yelled against the clattering of the tracks and the boom of the whistle. "You are a coward!" I didn't even know if he could hear me but it didn't matter. I believed he was gone to me, although I could still see him down the tracks, I believed him to be as good as gone.

I watched another train go by me, charging down the track closest them. How they knew it would be the one to take to Toronto, I did not know. As it passed them, moving slowly, Jimmy threw up his sack and began running. He climbed into the open box car and reached out his hand to my brother who had been keeping pace. I saw Charlie throw up his bag but I turned my eyes and began bawling into my hands. I did not want to see him gone. I wanted to open my eyes and be back in my bed, where I would have been on any normal Saturday morning.

***

I walked in the back door, not expecting anyone to be awake but found a room full of faces looking at me from the breakfast table. Mama was standing next to the kettle, her apron on as it was every morning. Pa was seated at the head of the table, but he was not reading the paper as usual. It lay untouched beside him. I glanced to Mary who only hung her head towards her porridge. She had told them but I could hardly blame her.

"Where's Charlie?" my father asked, poking at the inside of his cheek with his tongue. I swallowed hard as everyone looked to me.

"He's in the shed," I answered earnestly, "getting the papers ready."

As if on cue, the shed door slammed. My father nodded and turned his attention to his paper. My mother gave a slight smile and turned back to the stove. I could have sworn I saw a tear, as if they had known where we were. Why no one came out to stop him I'll never know. Perhaps they knew nothing could be done, or perhaps they felt if anything could be done I was the one to do it.

***

The thundering of the train petered away becoming more and more distant the longer I cried into my hands. I waited for what felt like forever until I knew the train was completely gone and the track would be empty. I forced myself to look up, not wanting to see the empty tracks but reconciled myself to the task of telling Mama and Pa about Charlie's biggest mistake.

My tear blurred eyes were playing tricks on me. I thought I saw Charlie walking along the track.

Walking back to me.

It was impossible. I had seen him reaching out his hand to board the train. I saw him throw up his sack. Yet there he was sauntering down the track, his hands thrust in his pockets. I saw him glance once over his shoulder, possibly thinking of his one chance to get away and cursing himself for inviting his damn sister along to say goodbye. But perhaps that's the way he planned it all along as a way of saving face with his friend.

***

I didn't dare to speak of the day when Charlie almost left, at least not until we found ourselves standing on the train station platform not five years later. Charlie was wearing his uniform, collected from the recruitment office the day before. He was leaving, with a ticket this time. He could not change his mind no matter how much his little sister pleaded.

He hugged Mama and Pa before turning to me, a broad smile spreading across his face. "Don't try to talk me out of it," he said, wrapping his arms around me.

He watched me, as if hesitating, waiting for my words of wisdom.

"You are the bravest man I know," I said. "You're very courageous... Charlie Meyer."

The train whistle blew over us and the conductor yelled from his step the familiar call. The train would be leaving and we needed to say goodbye.

Charlie ruffled the hair on Jacob's head, and hugged Mary tightly. Before he boarded the train Pa slapped him on the back and nodded his approval. I wondered if anyone else could see the tears for all the pride. My brother waved to us once more before disappearing in the passenger car. We saw him in the window just briefly before the train began to pull away from the platform.

We never saw him again. He died in the fight for France. Mama was in the garden and I was seated on the porch reading. I looked up when I saw the uniformed messenger making his way up the walk. I had been smiling over a passage I had just read but my smile faded when I saw him hand the telegram over to my mother's garden soiled fingers.

He was gone. I knew in that moment and no one needed to tell me. He was gone.

Some years later the grain elevator closed its doors. The trains became less frequent before stopping altogether. The train station operates as a museum now with a small portion of track remaining where miles and miles used to begin.

I paid a visit there once and could have sworn I saw him, Charlie, on the end of the platform waving his goodbye, my mind making the switch from fourteen to twenty in a matter of seconds. Over the years my mind confused the two memories until they seemed to melt into one. Some days I feel as if I said goodbye to my brother twice, each time never seeing or hearing from him again.

About Tracy L. Ward

Tracy L. Ward is the author of *Chorus of the Dead*, the first book in a Victorian morgue mystery series featuring surgeon, Peter Ainsley, now available on Kindle and Kobo. A journalist by trade, Tracy enjoyed numerous bylines in both newspapers and magazines before embarking on her journey into fiction.

Visit Tracy at her BlogSpot
http://www.gothicmysterywriter.blogspot.ca/
or at her Amazon Author Page

THE MINSTREL'S SPELL

Susan M. Botich

Long ago, near a small village by a vast wood, there once lived a humble farmer and his wife.

They had but one child, a girl of sturdy build with a flat, round face. Those who were kind called her plain. Others, with cruel hearts, would carelessly claim that she was the ugliest child ever born. She was a good child and kind-hearted, but still the neighbors would whisper that she was so ugly no man would ever possibly want her.

The child's name was Edith. Her mother and father were devoted to her as she was to them. She treated all the creatures on or near the small farm as her friends, for she had no one else to play with. Accept for when the occasional rude remark was said behind her back, Edith was a happy child. She and her family lived a quiet, but contented life. And that was how she grew into womanhood.

Now in the village there lived a widowed carpenter who had but one son, who he called Jack. He was large and broad with a strong back, small, round eyes, large nose and very full lips. Many people in the village muttered to each other as he passed them on the street. They called him dumb and clumsy because of his appearance, yet he was neither. He was quite skilled despite his youth and could, in fact, out do his father in any aspect of their profession.

One autumn, as the gold leaves were beginning to turn brown, Edith's mother became ill. She would not regain her strength and finally, one cold grey morning, she died. The young girl's father was so heart-broken, he too fell ill and, just before the winter snows thawed, he quietly passed away, leaving the farm to his dear daughter.

Edith was now a grown woman and filled with loneliness at the loss of both her mother and father within the same year. She managed the farm alone but, as a few years passed, it became too much. The little house, along with the barn and the fences, were all in much need of repair and she couldn't manage it alone. So, as much as she disliked going to the village (for there were always smirks and nasty comments said about her behind her back), she decided to seek out a carpenter there.

She left for the village the very next day. She arrived midmorning, not stopping to talk to anyone, but going straight to the small carpenter's shop. She entered the shop a little timidly. Seeing no one there, she decided to wait. After what seemed like a long time, she began to wonder if the carpenter was out for the day and had forgotten to lock up. Just as she was turning to leave, there appeared a large, broad man with carpenter's belt standing half in the shadows of the doorway.

"How may I help you, Ma'am?" his deep, throaty voice asked. His manner was gentle and, while he stood, he shuffled his feet a little bashfully. For the first time since her parent's had died, while standing in the presence of another, Edith didn't feel ugly.

She answered him in a soft, calm voice even though she was a little nervous.

"Master Carpenter, I've come to hire a worker for repairs on my house and barn and the fences too, if it's not too much trouble. You see both my mother and my father are dead and I've been managing the farm alone, but it's become too much for me this past year. I can pay you promptly when work is completed!"

The young carpenter stepped into the shop and out of the shadows.

"I am not the Master Carpenter. I am his son. My name is Jack and, if you like, I can come tomorrow to begin the work."

Jack smiled a little shyly at Edith. He usually didn't feel comfortable around others, but this young woman was different. She was short and squat with a broad face, but she seemed good-hearted to him and he felt compassion for her, having lost both her parents.

At that moment, the old master carpenter entered the shop and stood just inside the doorway, looking at Edith and then his son and then back at Edith again.

"What's this?" the old man asked with a curious look.

Jack hadn't heard his father come in behind him. In fact, both Jack and Edith were startled a little at the intrusion.

"Father," Jack began in his husky voice, "this young woman needs some repairs done on her place. I told her I could begin tomorrow, since we've just finished the last job."

Jack's father was a little irritated that his son had arranged to take a job on his own, without first consulting him, but he knew it was only a matter of time before Jack would either take over the shop or go off on his own. He couldn't expect his son to act as though he were an apprentice forever.

"I see," replied the old man. "Very well. Tomorrow it is then"

Early the next morning Jack arrived at the farm. He worked carefully on each task that Edith put before him. He found himself wanting to please her with his work and something more than that. He simply wanted to please her.

They talked together quite easily whenever they were working near each other. Edith began to look for chores that needed to be done near Jack just to be close to him. They would talk and laugh over the midday meal Edith set.

Each following day was spent this way until, finally, the last of the repairs was completed. The day's end was growing near and Edith watched Jack slowly put each tool carefully away. Then, as she drew nearer to him, bringing the money she owed him, he noticed her sadness. His heart felt deeply touched by her. Never had anyone caused him so much joy and sorrow at the same time. He asked her if he might see her again and her smile overtook her homely face, making it seem beautiful.

They agreed to see each other often, and beamed their good-byes to one another. Jack kept turning to look back and waved again and again every few steps. His heart felt as light as a bubbling brook.

Jack and Edith kept their promises to one another as often as they could. He would come to see her at her little farm and she found she needed to visit the village quite often now, each time stopping at the small carpenter's shop. Their fondness grew into love and one warm summer's evening Jack asked Edith to be his wife. They were soon wed near her farm in a large meadow full of wildflowers and honeysuckle.

***

Jack and Edith lived happily together on the little farm. Each day Jack walked the distance into the village to work with his father. He had hoped his father would come to live with them, but he was a stubborn man and not easily taken to change. He had grown accustomed to his tiny rooms behind the little shop and so, for a time, his father stayed in the village. More and more the old carpenter would take the smaller projects, leaving the more difficult ones to Jack. His back was a little more bent than it used to be and he needed to take rest more often than before.

As time went by, Jack developed a name for himself as a master craftsman, as well as builder. Now, those who came to the little shop asked for him directly, with all due respect to the old Master Carpenter.

Edith made sure that her father-in-law was kept well-fed, always sending along baskets of fresh baked bread, eggs, cheese, and vegetables with her husband. She worried about the old man, but he seemed happy enough and would come to visit them occasionally when he could. And so they spent their days, contented with their lives.

Much had changed for Jack and Edith, but one thing remained as it had always been. The smirks and whispers behind their backs as they walked the village streets, didn't lessen. Now the neighbors gossiped even more. They declared how it was a stroke of good fortune the couple didn't have any children. What on earth would the children of two people like that look like? They would surely be hideous! People like that shouldn't have children, anyway....and so on, and so on.

The one thing that amazed the Master Carpenter was that no one ever seemed to notice or comment on how good and kind his children were. Although he kept to himself now, he would still occasionally overhear the ridicule and it caused his heart to grow very heavy. After a few years, It began to wear the old man down. He resented the shallow, cold hearts of his neighbors. He finally closed the shop up and went to live the rest of his days on the farm with his son and daughter-in-law.

As the years passed by, Jack and Edith saw people less and less. They visited the village as little as possible. Those who sought out Jack for hire would customarily meet with his father to make the arrangements. Jack had asked his father to take on this task out of respect for the old man who could now only handle the easier work. His father had heartily agreed because he had watched the hurt on Jack's face when people would squirm and grimace in poorly concealed disgust at the sight of his son.

Now one day, as twilight neared, a young man in humble clothes appeared from around the road's bend. He looked to be a traveler, by way of the few belongings strapped to his back, and his weary gait. He approached Jack, who had been working in the field and had just stopped to look up from his labor to take in the beauty of the sunset. At first he didn't speak, but stood in silence with Jack, gazing with appreciation at the changing colors that played upon the sky. When finally the evening embraced them, the stranger broke the silence.

"Kind farmer," he began, "I am a traveling minstrel and in need of a place to sleep for the night. Although I am accustomed to making the earth my bed, if you would be kind enough to let me sleep in your barn, I will entertain you with song and story this evening as payment. I am quite skilled and have been found by many to be very amusing."

"You are very welcome to stay the night in our barn and your songs and stories will be welcomed too!" Jack graciously replied. "I'm about to go in for supper. You are also welcome to join us."

The stranger smiled and nodded and followed Jack into the cozy little house. At first Edith and her father-in-law looked surprised and a little distrustful of the stranger. But, after Jack explained, they greeted the young man warmly and invited him to sit down and join them.

At first there was an uncomfortable silence. They were used to people avoiding them and didn't know quite how to take the casual friendship of the stranger. But, as the young man began to tell them of his travels, where he'd been and what he'd seen, they soon relaxed and were grateful for the company. The quiet stranger told them stories that made them laugh and sometimes shake their heads in awe or disbelief, for not one of them had been farther than the country outside the small village.

After supper, they all gathered near the fire and the stranger pulled out a small lap harp from its tattered bag. He began to play a haunting tune that held the three in a captive spell. Then, slowly and sweetly, he began to sing. They listened in astonishment as his song told the story of their very own lives. It told of the scorn shown them because of their appearance. It told of their love for each other, but of the loneliness in their hearts too. It told of their goodness, gentle spirits, and of the kindness they showed others throughout the years. Then he sang of how one sweet spring evening a traveling stranger came to ask for a place to sleep for the night and, because of their kindness toward him, they would be given a special gift in return. And the gift that would be given them was this; that, within one year's time, both Jack and Edith would be transformed into the most pleasing to behold in all the land.

As he sang his enchanting song, tears welled up in the eyes of the old man, for he loved his children dearly, and, as he wept, he fell into a deep, dreamless sleep.

***

When the old man awoke the next morning, he asked Jack and Edith about the young visitor and the very beautiful, enchanting song. They remembered no such song and told him it must have been a dream he had. He insisted it was not a dream, but a spell cast over them by the strange young minstrel. They patiently listened to him, but gently denied their father's story. They explained that the young man went to bed after supper and had left early before dawn's first light. They urged their beloved father to put it behind him and think of it no more.

Now, as the year drew on, and their love only deepened, Jack and Edith began to notice a change taking place in one another. Edith was losing her homely, squat appearance and was beginning to look as graceful and lovely as any woman could be. Jack began to look handsome and sure of himself. They began to quietly discuss among themselves the night the stranger had come to visit them, and even wondered if the story their father had told them could possibly be true.

Day after day, spring into summer and summer into fall, they watched the mysterious transformation unfold. Finally, after the long, hard, cold winter loosed its grip and spring flowers began to bloom, Jack and Edith were struck with a wonderful idea!

They decided to invite everyone they'd ever known to come and share a special spring celebration with them! No one knew that the two ugly outcasts had now become the handsomest couple in all the land and that would be their surprise!

They were very excited about their plan but, when they told their father, he only shook his head with doubt. He feared his children would only be hurt even more deeply by this folly, for, to his old eyes, they hadn't changed at all. The old man did, however, finally agree to send word to the village and the surrounding area about Jack and Edith's spring feast.

Jack and Edith busied themselves to prepare for the special event. There was so much to be done and they were very excited! Edith's lavender and wild roses graced the arbor around the house. Honeysuckle released its sweet perfume all around the yard. Every window sill had flower pots full of bright daisies. When the day of the festival came, they were ready. There would be mutton and hams, boiled eggs, fresh vegetables, apples, and pastries. They worked very hard to make it the most wonderful celebration ever seen!

In late morning, on the appointed day, people began to arrive. Jack and Edith remained hidden in their room while their father greeted one and all. They wanted to make a grand entrance after all the guests had arrived. Dressed in their finest, they giggled with excitement at the thought of how surprised everyone would be to see them.

"They probably won't even recognize us," they whispered to each other.

The guests chattered and laughed among themselves about the strange couple. Most had come simply for the free feast. Some out of curiosity, for there had been a hint of mystery with the invitation.

Jack's father served wine to the guests and tried to ignore the snickers and whispers he couldn't help but overhear. He dreaded the outcome of the day, but did as his children asked, for he couldn't bear to break their hearts with the truth. It was his last hope that people would be kind after all, but now his hopes fell.

Then a very strange thing happened. The young minstrel who had visited them the spring before, suddenly appeared in the midst of the guests. He pulled his harp from its tattered bag and began to play and amuse everyone. There was much laughter and dancing and no one gave a thought to Jack and Edith. The old carpenter watched and wondered at this but said nothing.

After a while, everyone grew very tired and, one by one, they all laid down right where they had stood and fell asleep. Only the old man remained awake. Amazed, he approached the young minstrel and stood before him.

"How is this?" he asked in awe and wonder.

"First you visit our house one year ago in the spring and I dream of a spell cast over my children. Then I watch in anguish as they begin to believe that they have been transformed into Beauty itself. For love of them, I said nothing. But now this? Have you woven your magic once more? And to what end this time? I beg you now, Stranger," the old man pleaded, "to leave us and never again return."

The minstrel smiled and, without a word, left the farm, never to return.

The old man went to the room where his children waited. He knocked on the door and Jack opened it. He and Edith stood ready to make their planned appearance. The old man just stood silent, not knowing what to tell them. Suddenly, every guest began to stir and arise.

Jack and Edith began to slowly make their way through the crowd, greeting each one as they would pass. There was a murmuring throughout the house and yard as each and everyone gazed with astonishment at them.

"They're beautiful!" some exclaimed.

"Is it really them?" others whispered.

"Has magic been cast upon this house?" others wondered out loud.

As Jack and Edith passed by and the guests would turn to speak amongst themselves, each and every one of them began to see each other very differently. They began to see their own ugliness for how they had treated these gracious folk over the years. For the first time, they began to feel ashamed and heart-sick.

Then, as the old man looked on in astonishment, one by one, each guest came forward, admitted to their wrongs and, very humbly, asked for forgiveness!

The beautiful couple graciously accepted all the apologies and nearly wept for joy at the thought that, finally, they might have friends. They held not one hard feeling against all their neighbors. It had never been their way to harden their hearts.

The old man just shook his head and smiled to himself. Jack and Edith hadn't changed at all. They were the same as they'd always been. But the minstrel had, indeed, cast a spell. For all who beheld them would see them as they truly were. They had always been beautiful in their hearts. Never again did one person utter an unkind word about Jack or Edith. For the rest of their days, everyone who beheld them treated them as though they were a prince and princess living among them.

One year passed from the time of the spring celebration and Edith and Jack were blessed with the first of their five children. All in all, they had three fine sons and two lovely daughters that gave them joy for the rest of their days.

The old carpenter never said a word to anyone about the minstrel's magic, but lived out the remainder of his life as a quietly contented man. In fact, he was often seen chuckling to himself with a look of uncontrolled amusement.

About Susan M. Botich

Susan M. Botich is a storyteller. She tells her stories through songs, poems, short stories, and novels. She lives in Bend, Oregon, with her exceptionally innovative husband.

Visit Susan at her Website
http://www.susanbotich.com/
or look for her titles at Amazon

THE LEGEND OF THE CORKSCREW SWAMP

Dayna Leigh Cheser

On February first, 2003, I deposited a nice bonus check and took a leave of absence from the real estate firm in New York City where I'd had an exceptional year as a Broker/Associate. Now, it was family time. My wife and I packed our five kids into our Lexus, and made for warm and sunny Florida.

We spent two weeks working our way down the east coast. After the Jacksonville/St. Augustine area, our next stop was the Daytona 500 where, on February sixteenth, Michael Waltrip won the race. The next stop was Orlando and Disney World.

Next, we went to Sea World, which I thought was great, and the Space Center, even better, then visited family in the Ft. Lauderdale/Miami area.

One day, we stood on Smathers Beach, near the western end of Route A1A on Key West, looking out over the vast expanse of ocean around us – the Gulf of Mexico to the west and the Atlantic Ocean to the east.

Back on the mainland, we drove west across Alligator Alley, now a four-lane Interstate with fences to keep the alligators off the road. The kids scanned the roadside canals, hoping to see some of the prehistoric creatures.

I, on the other hand, a city-boy all my life, became

concerned about the total absence of civilization. We were crossing the Everglades, the Sea of Grass. Exits were few and only one gas station/convenience mart appeared during the two-hour drive.

At the first Naples exit, I turned off the highway, eager for civilization again. We found a great hotel on the beach, and watched the sun set into the Gulf of Mexico. Soon, the soothing sounds of the waves slapping the beach lulled us to sleep.

At first light, the kids were up and ready to go. We selected interesting brochures from a display in the lobby, including one for a place called 'The Corkscrew Swamp Sanctuary,' an Audubon Society property, inland and northeast of the city.

Nearly an hour later, we stopped for gas. While I was filling up, a battered old pickup truck pulled in and parked in front of the convenience store, not far from where I stood.

"Excuse me, sir," I called to the old man who emerged from the truck. "Excuse me," I repeated, a bit louder.

The old man turned and shuffled over, removing his cap and wiping his brow with his sleeve as he walked. His hair was grey and sparse but his blue eyes were bright.

"Hi!" I began, a little uncomfortable under his gaze. "Uh, how far it is to the Corkscrew Swamp Sanctuary? I'm afraid I might have missed it."

"Nope. It's still a few miles that way, on the left," he said. His gaze softened and he smiled. Something about him changed as he started to tell me a story.

Hypnotized, I listened. The busy convenience store and gas pumps faded away as he spoke. His story wove a rich tapestry in my mind; his words painting vivid pictures, almost like memories. I was transported to another world.

***

Billy Joe and his friends, Carlito, and Rain were bored. The summer break from school was almost over. Soon, they'd be back in school, with a different kind of boredom.

Sittings on old tree stumps, the trio watched Rain's mother hang laundry on a line strung between two trees and propped up by forked sticks. The sounds of summer formed the framework of their thoughts in the summer heat. The pines sighed and palmetto fronds chattered in the occasional breeze.

Billy Joe kicked his stump, his sneakers making soft, rhythmic thuds on the dead wood. Carlito wiped sweat from his face with a big red handkerchief. Rain, the youngest, tossed her long, black hair back over her shoulders. Billy Joe's mind wandered as he scanned the pines and palmetto landscape, hoping for inspiration.

The trio considered everything within bicycle range to be their private domain. The matter of warning signs, locked gates and even parental admonishments meant little to these young adventurers. Then, Billy Joe's eyes focused on a distant sign at the edge of the main road – 'the Corkscrew Swamp Sanctuary.'

"Yes!" he breathed. "The Swamp." The coming night was now ripe with the promise of excitement and adventure.

Billy Joe's friends looked at him, their eyes bright with anticipation. Carlito, a newcomer to the neighborhood, leaned closer, eyes wide. "What es 'swamp'?" His accent made his question difficult to understand.

Rain pondered a moment. "Pantano," she translated.

Carlito understood. "Ah, pantano, gracias."

She continued. "At the end of the road there's a place

called the Corkscrew Swamp. People pay to go there to look at plants and animals, birds mostly, but sometimes other stuff, too, like 'gators."

Billy Joe scoffed. "It's no fun there in the daytime. My cousin told me it's really scary at night. He's been there." Lowering his voice and leaning closer to his friends, he glanced toward Rain's mother, and challenged them. "If we go there tonight, after dark, we'll see if he's right."

Rain hushed the others. With her serious Seminole wisdom, she noted, "My mother has the ears of an eagle. If we do this, we must be very quiet." They nodded and resumed their bored stance.

Billy Joe kicked the dead stump; Carlito wiped sweat from his face with his handkerchief and Rain tossed her long hair back over her shoulders.

After supper and chores, the three friends met again at the stumps. Feigning boredom again, they watched as the red sun dropped below the horizon. Then, melting into the evening shadows, they made their way down the dusty dirt road to the Corkscrew Swamp Sanctuary entrance. The three friends didn't have mischief in mind, only the heart-pounding knowledge they would be someplace they shouldn't. Talking in subdued tones, they gained entry by climbing the gate and dropping to the ground inside. A full moon showed them the way.

Daytime visitors to the Corkscrew Swamp Sanctuary enter through a Welcome Center, and walk along a path through tall pines and palmetto ground cover before stepping out onto a boardwalk and into another world. In the moonlight, the scene took on a life of its own; instead of a wooden bridge-like structure, it became a gleaming silver path, straight at first, then winding around majestic cypress trees, old beyond years, before disappearing into the dark strand. The bright moon reflected off the surface of the still, shallow waters, illuminating the ripples created by frogs, bugs and other creatures of the night. The adventure was at hand.

The children, fearless in their youth, stepped out onto the boardwalk. They paused, then, laughing aloud, they took off at a run. Moments later, they stood where the boardwalk entered the dark cypress strand. Looking back, they saw the reflected moon and the pines beyond. Turning, they looked into the darkness ahead. What awaited them there?

The three stood transfixed by the endless possibilities. Rain, the tiny Seminole brave, broke the spell with a toss of her head. Laughing, she poked her friends, and set off into the darkness. Billy Joe and Carlito followed close behind her.

What befell the trio on that fateful night will never be known. While it was undeniably dark, and, could be dangerous, whatever was inside the dark strand whisked them away without a trace. Billy Joe, Carlito and Rain were never found.

Friends and family spent agonizing weeks looking for them before the authorities finally called off the search. It is said that on still, summer nights, when the moon is full, if you listen closely, you might hear Billy Joe, Carlito and Rain laughing.

***

The old man stopped talking. Without a word, he turned and shuffled into the store. I shook my head and blinked. The moonlit boardwalk faded away, the nocturnal quiet transformed to traffic noise; the primordial cypress strand became a busy convenience store parking lot. As awareness returned, I realized my wife and kids were clamoring for me to finish and get going. I put the nozzle back in the pump and collected the receipt.

As I got into the car, I stopped, struck by a flash of insight. Was the old man Billy Joe? In the rear view mirror, I saw he had emerged from the store. I got out of the car to ask him, but his truck was pulling away. Jumping back into my car, I turned to follow him; but the truck had vanished.

Sighing, I turned toward Corkscrew Swamp. I wondered *why* he'd told me the story. Then, I saw things as he saw them. Clearly, we weren't 'natives.' So, was this a 'legend' perpetrated on unsuspecting tourists? If so, it never really happened and the old man couldn't be Billy Joe. I smiled, chuckling to myself.

The story stuck in my mind, though. It wasn't long before my wife and I were standing right where the children in the old man's story had stood that fateful night, at the edge of the boardwalk. The daylight faded away. I saw the full moon reflecting on the water. In the distance, at the edge of the strand, I saw Billy Joe, Carlito and Rain.

My wife nudged me. "Honey, come on! The kids are way ahead of us." The sun beat down, bright and warm. Blinking, I saw my kids, right at the edge of the strand, where Billy Joe, Carlito and Rain had stood. A shiver went down my spine. We hurried to catch up. Together, we entered the cool, dim strand.

We saw the wonders of this unique, subtropical swamp, and had a special treat. In one of the lettuce lakes, there were alligators. Several were sunning themselves on small hammocks, while others prowled the waters. With only their snouts and eyes breaking the surface of the water, they barely caused a wake as they moved with great stealth. I stood on the boardwalk leaning on the rail, watching the ancient reptiles.

One of the 'gators glided close to where I stood. In its eyes, I could almost see back to when the Earth was young, and 'gators, not so much different from the creature before me, searched for meals, perhaps here, in this place. We stared at each other for what seemed like an eternity. Then, without a sound, the 'gator submerged into the dark water. It disappeared, like Billy Joe, Carlito and Rain.

The afternoon we spent at the Corkscrew Swamp Sanctuary was the highlight of our vacation. Much to my surprise, the kids want to go back again. Someday, we will. I'll never forget the old man and his tale of youth and adventure, even if it wasn't true. Or was it?

Years later, I still think of the 'legend.' Was it really just for tourists or was it a true story? When I think about it, I get the same feeling I'd had at the gas pump - there was something otherworldly about the old man.

About Dayna Leigh Cheser

Author Dayna Leigh Cheser is a life-long reader/writer. After retiring, she 'got serious' and published her debut novel, *Janelle's Time*, an adult historical romance, in 2012. Four more books in the *TIME* series will soon follow. She currently lives in southwest Florida with her husband, Peter, and her cat, Spunkie.

Visit her at her Website
http://aplaceforwriters.wordpress.com/
or at her FaceBook Page

THE MIGHTY PEN

Troy L. Lambert

My grandfather never wrote anything down. He always committed everything to memory. I asked him why once and he simply said this:

"Boy, the pen is mightier than the sword. You don't want to trust a dullard like me with a weapon that powerful."

My grandfather had a sixth grade education. He had quit school to help his father on the farm, and all along I figured that writing was just a hardship for him. Grandpa even did math in his head. He never even wrote a grocery list. I never found out why until a sunny day in 1995.

I walked into the nursing home where grandpa was sitting in a rocker looking out the window. In his hand was a pen. In front of him was a notebook.

"What are you doing Grandpa?" I asked. Grandpa did not answer. He seldom did these days. I figured his talking days were almost done. I never dreamed he would start writing instead. The memory of yesteryear was gone: I figured that is where the stories had gone too.

He held the pen tightly. When I asked him the question again, he began to scribble on the pad. "Just sitting," he scrawled. The penmanship was surprisingly neat, the letters clearly formed.

"Thought you didn't write, Grandpa," I said. I admit I had a little smirk. My grandfather and I had made a game of making fun of each other over the years. I was trying to spark that again. I never would have if I had known then what I know now.

Outside the window a dog was barking incessantly. There were a couple of kids out there playing with it, laughing and giggling.

Grandpa started to scrawl on the paper again. "I wish that dog would shut up," he wrote.

I laughed. It was suddenly so like him—he hated dogs that barked constantly and had chased people from his neighborhood when they would walk such dogs near his house. He would grin, playing the role of a crazy old man. It was a role anyone who knew him knew he did not fit. He was not crazy. I swear to you he wasn't.

Outside the dog yelped. Grandpa's hand started to tremble. The dog jumped still trying to enjoy the game, and yelped again as he landed. A little girl screamed. The dog fell on its side, writhing in the grass. White froth came from its mouth, and I saw a parent rush from the corner of my vision and try to comfort the children and grab the dog at the same time.

I was distracted by all the commotion, but when I turned to look back at grandpa he was crying. I had never seen him cry before, and in his still powerful right hand the pen was crushed. In crushing the pen he had cut his hand, and ink and blood mingled on the wheel of his chair and puddled on the floor.

It wasn't the pain. Grandpa's eyes showed grief. He wasn't crying. He was weeping in sorrow. Suddenly a memory came flooding in and I realized I had seen him cry once before exactly like this. It was the day my grandmother died.

***

April 1, 1990. April Fool's Day had brought with it spring, even if we knew it would be short lived this far north, and winter likely had another month up her sleeve. My grandmother was still healthy as could be at seventy-eight and showed no signs of slowing down. Grandpa was not yet in a wheelchair, but his legs were going. A weakness had settled there, and he did not do nearly as much walking as he had before.

We loaded him in his van and took him out to our favorite fishing hole. We had been going there since we were small children. A new pier had been constructed and it had handicap access. All the places we had hiked along the river to fish were to be no more for Grandpa. This was now his spot: it was almost as if it had been created just for him.

April was before the standard fishing season, but the pier stretched over the Snake River: rivers were technically open to fishing all year. We didn't expect much. The trout would be sluggish and likely not into the spring feeding frenzy yet. It was a chance for grandpa—for all of us—to get out and spend time in the sun.

Grandpa was still telling stories at that point. As the sun rose and the air got warm jackets were shed and hung over rails. Worms were drowned. The coffee thermos was empty and the water bottles were fetched from the cooler by either my brother or I.

There was a silence. There had been no bites—the poles were as unmoving as the spring air. That is why we thought the story was a joke.

"It was a day like this," he started. "The water still too cold, but the air so warm we couldn't sit in the house and stare at the walls any more. Dad took us out fishin'. This was on the Platte in Nebraska, long before we lived here. I was about ten or so. Old enough to know better."

He paused and sipped some water. None of us had heard this tale before, but I looked at Grandma and could tell that she had. Usually when she had heard a tale of his before she showed an indifferent lack of interest. This time she had a look of utter fear on her face as if he was about to reveal an ancient secret.

"I already knew I was different from the other boys. I was about a year from quittin' school and helpin' dad on the farm. But I had no idea about that then." He span into the dirt. "I knew that I had a knack for getting' what I wanted. I just didn't quite know how things worked yet.

"My dad told me we weren't going to catch a thing. It was too early. He had about enough of us boys wrestling in the living room, and I think he was afraid my ma would beat us to death with the broom if we broke one more of her good dishes or her figurines throwin' a ball in the house. Kinda like what used to happen to you and your brother Bill." He pointed to me. "You remember your momma on those days dontcha?"

I said I did.

"Well, my momma was no different than yours. Little meaner maybe. Anyhow so he hustled us out of the house and took us down to the river. The water was still brown and slow and he thought the fish were still sleepin'.

"'You'll catch one if you hit it on the head, and tick it off enough to bite whatever hit it,' he told us.

"I figured he was right. He knew most of the time what he was talking about when it came to fishin' and huntin'. He had kinda an instinct for it. Kinda like the one I got right here."

He paused. He wiped his eyes, and I thought it was because he was tired. But I think looking back he was remembering the good old days. Those with his dad and his brother out on that river.

"I wanted to catch fish though. I wanted a big ole catfish for ma to fry up for supper. I wanted the days of summer that were not yet here. I wished real hard, because back then I still thought that might be enough sometimes. It wasn't. I started singin'.

"Fishy, fishy in the brook," his voice rose. "Come and bite on Grandpa's hook. I will catch you if I can. Cook you in a fryin' pan."

It was something we had all heard him sing before. We all smiled. All of us except for Grandma. She frowned as if she knew what was next.

"Of course that did nothing. Dad even made fun of me. 'Son, wish in one hand and crap in the other. See which one fills up first.' Dad had his pole stuck in one of those rod holder stakes you stick deep into the mud. We didn't buy 'em back then. We made 'em with PVC pipe and parts of old fence posts.

"I finally took a little notepad from my pocket and the stub of a pencil. I wrote in big letters on the pad 'three big catfish.'

"You have to understand I did not know at the time that wishin' for stuff like that had consequences. As I put a period at the end of that simple sentence, dad's pole bent near in half with a bite. He grabbed it and I could see his strong arms straining to hold it as line sped out of his reel with a high pitched whine.

"My pole followed his. So did my brother's. We had three big cats on at once. My brother was younger and he was struggling not to get dragged into the river. I stood my ground, but it was tough. My arms were straining. I saw my little brother to my right lay on his back and put his feet agin a stump to hold himself from slidin' through the mud.

"Dad got his fish pulled up on the shore and put a gaffing hook into its brain right away. He knew if he didn't kill that fish it might flop all over and hurt somebody. He had two more fish to deal with. He jumped over to help my bother Mikey, yellin' at me to just hang on.

"Moments later, but what seemed like an eternity to a little boy with sore arms and a sore back, he had landed Mikey's fish and killed it as well. 'Here you are Eddie,' he told me grabbin' my rod. I collapsed to the muddy bank and rubbed my sore arms as he pulled.

"I shoulda' seen it comin'. I didn't and dad was tired by this point. Mikey was young and curious. He was way too excited and payin' too little attention. I moved out the way as dad pulled in that last fish but Mikey didn't."

There was quiet on the pier and we knew this story wasn't gonna end with a punch line. This was one of Grandpa's true stories.

"Dad swung the gaffing hook one more time, intendin' to kill the last fish. Then I figured to haul all of this up to the house he would have to go get the tractor. The bank was a bit muddy for the truck yet. Mikey was behind him but too close. The hook stuck in Mikey's hand and drug him forward. Dad felt the resistance and thought he hooked a limb or bush behind him. He pulled harder, tossin' Mikey on top of that big cat."

"Is that how Great Uncle Mike. . ."

"Yeah, Eddie that is how he lost his hand. My fault. I wished for fish, and I got 'em. But there was a cost. There is always a cost when you wish for something'."

"Careful what you wish for and all that. Know what happened to those fish?"

We all shook our heads. All but Grandma.

"They rotted on that bank. It was fifty miles to the nearest hospital that could fix Mikey's hand. We dang near didn't make it in time to save Mikey. Lucky I thought somethin' worked once that day and it might work again.

"On the way I wrote in my notebook: 'I wish my brother will be okay' and he was. If only I had known I would have wished his hand would be okay too. I have no idea what the consequences of that might have been."

"So are you telling us Grandpa that if you wish for something, you get it?" my brother asked.

"If I write it down," Grandpa said. "Only if I write it down."

Bill laughed. The rest of us joined him nervously. I wasn't sure if Grandpa was being funny at this point or not. He reddened but remained quiet.

Grandma watched in disturbing silence.

***

The following week she was killed in a car accident. She had gone out to the store in the van and decided to go to the market at the end of town. They had better meat, but you had to cross the highway to get there. As she pulled out to cross she was struck broadside by a semi that had lost his brakes coming down the huge pass just before their small town.

The state police said he was going almost a hundred miles an hour, and was totally out of control. She died instantly.

At the funeral Grandpa wept. That was when I had seen him cry like he was now in the nursing home.

"My fault, my fault," he kept saying that day.

I hugged him. I was always close to him. "Careful what you wish for," he whispered in my ear. Even then, I think he knew.

***

I remembered the story as they bandaged up his hand. I was trying to sort in my head what it might mean. A pickup truck had pulled up and the body of the dog was gone. The family had long since fled.

"When did he start writing?" I asked the nurse.

"Last week. He was having such trouble

communicating the speech therapist thought this might do him some good. He seemed happy with it the first couple of days. What happened?"

"I am not sure," I lied. I thought I just might know.

Grandpa looked at me. I could tell he had something to say. With his uninjured left had he gestured like he wanted to write. I looked around and found a pad and the stub of a pencil. He took the pencil awkwardly in his left fist and scrawled on the paper I held for him. There was only one word.

"D-I-A-R-Y," the ugly capital letters read.

I patted his hand and he smiled, sitting back into his chair. He knew I understood what he wanted me to look for.

Grandpa had kept a diary, and I needed to find it. It was 1995. Grandma had been dead for five years, and Grandpa looked like he might follow her at any time. I had just discovered that my Grandpa did write.

***

There was not one diary. There were four notebooks all filled with close, neat handwriting that I never would have suspected from him. I took them to the kitchen table of the house he no longer lived in, and sat down to read.

The entries were short. The first page of the oldest simply said "I must be careful what I wish for."

"May 17, 1935: I wish Elna liked me more."

The page across from the entry held a newspaper clipping. "Football Star Drowns." I shivered and turned the page.

"August 7, 1935: I wish Elna would agree to marry me."

The facing page held a birth announcement. February 28, 1936. A little girl born to Elna and Ed Ingram. I did some math quickly in my head, and figured why my

Grandmother had agreed to marry Grandpa.

"January 23, 1938: A son would be nice." A birth announcement on the facing page. Underneath, seemingly unrelated was an article about a hospital in a town nearly seventy miles from their home burning to the ground.

I flipped ahead a few pages. Each page seemed to have a wish, and a facing article or story. "September 11, 1949: I really would love a new house." The facing page held an article that I recognized from a story my mother had told me. A plane had crashed into their house when she was thirteen or so.

"It was just a crop duster. The pilot lost control and he was killed, along with half our cows. But we got a new house and more cows. Something about insurance."

The news article called the crash suspicious. There were no follow ups.

I skipped to the next book.

"August 29, 1960: I wish Kennedy was President. Even for a couple of years. I think he would do the country some good."

The facing page held an article about Kennedy's assassination. Under the original entry were scrawled the words "I AM A FOOL" in all capitals. 1963 was scrawled underneath. A few pages later:

"April 10, 1970: I wish we would stop wasting money going to the moon!"

The facing page held an article about Apollo 13. An oxygen tank exploding on takeoff. Underneath was scrawled: "Bring those men home safe!" The following page held an article on the miraculous safe return of Apollo to the Earth.

The rest of the notebook was blank. I sat back and sighed. I looked at the next two books. I wondered if Grandma had ever found these. Grandpa thought he controlled events by wishing. I began to wonder if he was right. I was exhausted but curiosity drew me to the other two books.

I opened the next. Inside the cover was written in his close hand the words "I must be more careful what I wish for." More was underlined twice.

By this time Grandpa had moved to Idaho. The kids were grown and scattered.

"February 28, 1971. I wish Samantha would come home to stay with us."

Samantha was my mother. On the facing page was an article that made my heart stop. "Local man killed in Vietnam: Wife returns to be with family." A faded picture in the newspaper showed my mother, my brother and I standing in front of an airplane. My grandpa had always tried to take my father's role in my life, but had always reminded me that he was not my dad.

"Your dad gave it all in that cursed war," he declared often. "Don't ever forget it."

I wanted to stop. I wanted to run to the nursing home and grab him up. I wanted to hug him and tell him all of these things were coincidences. That he could not have caused them all. That he could not blame himself. It just wasn't right.

Then I thought of the dog. The dog on the lawn. I flipped ahead.

"June 4, 1976: wish we had some dam water around here."

"The Teton Dam Breaks" declared the facing article.

"Learn to Spell!" he had written underneath.

"Library Receives Huge Shipment" a small article taped underneath read. The local library had received a huge shipment of dictionaries they were giving away.

I slammed the book shut. I was wondering who was

crazier. Him or me. He had believed he was doing all of these things, and had recorded them. After a few hours reading, and one incident with a dog, I believed him too.

Reluctantly I opened the last notebook. The front was filled but it was clear by looking that the articles stopped about halfway through.

"I must experiment, but carefully," the opening inscription read. The air in the house suddenly seemed to drop twenty degrees. I shuddered at the word "experiment."

The first page had a scrap of paper taped to it. The paper was a list titled "Grocery Wish List." It was simple. In big letters were written:

Coffee
Bread
Tea
Bacon
Eggs

Under these in my Grandmother's handwriting were two more items:

Oatmeal
Potatoes

The facing article was astounding: "Man Wins Grocery Raffle." I didn't need to read all of it because items in the article had been highlighted. "The bag he won contained Coffee, Bread, Tea, Bacon, and Eggs. 'I guess I have only two things to get,' his wife Elna Ingram declared. 'This is just what I wished for,' Eddie declared."

I didn't want to believe. It was such a small thing. A small coincidence but it was the small things that made no sense. A misspelling leading to a broken dam and a huge flood might be chocked up to accident or precognizant tendencies. A grocery raffle? With the exact items he wished for? Too much.

There was no article for the consequence of this experiment. Perhaps the little wishes had fewer consequences.

"This is crazy!" I said out loud. "It's not real!"

As I flipped the pages it became clearer that it was real. A wish for a new TV: an old friend passed away and left him his almost brand new set. "FOOL" was scratched on this page too. A wish for ice cream: a big rig crashed on main street spilling its load. Citizens were told to "take as much as they wished. It would never last to market now." The driver of the rig was critically injured, and died en-route to the hospital. A wish for a new church building: the old one burnt to the ground on a Sunday, injuring dozens.

"At least no one died," he had written under that one. I flipped to the last entry.

"April 8, 1990: I am afraid," the post read, "but I wish we had a new van. This one is falling apart."

There was no newspaper but I did not need one. My grandmother had died that day. A fiery crash on the highway on the way to the store. I looked out in the driveway at the five year old van with my pickup parked behind it. Five years ago it was a new van. I closed the books and started to weep, glad I was alone. When I got myself back under control I put the notebooks back where I had found them.

All the pages after that were blank. There was no more writing. No more wishes. It was no wonder Grandpa had never written anything down outside of these books. If he wrote it, it happened. He was probably terrified of what he might cause.

I thought then of the dog and Grandpa alone at the nursing home with an injured hand and a bloody pen. I was suddenly afraid of what he might write next.

I ran for the door.

***

Grandpa sat facing the window. The dog was gone: it was evening and suddenly I was hungry. I remembered I had not eaten all day. He heard me come in and smiled at me. On his tray was a notebook. Gripped clumsily in his left hand was the stub of a pencil.

"Did you find them?" he wrote awkwardly.

I nodded. I fought to keep the tears from my eyes, but seeing him they suddenly started to come.

He flipped back a page. "I wish Eddie would have dinner with me," he had written. He smiled at me.

"All you had to do was ask," I said, and wheeled him to the dining room.

We ate. The dinner consisted of overcooked meatloaf and canned green beans with instant mashed potatoes, something I usually could not stand. Tonight I ate them anyway. Grandpa ate with gusto as well.

"You should eat with him more often," the nurse said. "We can hardly get him to eat a thing."

I smiled. "Maybe I will."

If only I had known. If only I had flipped back to the page before, and seen what he had written there. I swear I would have stayed. It was written in pencil. Maybe I could have erased it. Maybe if I erased what he wrote, or even burned the page it wouldn't have happened.

But I wheeled him back to his room not knowing. I helped the nurses' aides put him to bed. I tucked him in and kissed his forehead like he had mine when I was a child. I put the notebook carefully in his night stand with his pencil. I turned out the light and walked away.

I can tell you I never forgot the way he looked as I walked out that night. He looked at peace. He looked like he had been carrying a burden and had finally set it down. Which I suppose in a way he had.

When they found him the next morning they told me he had just passed in his sleep. There was no reason for it. He hadn't suffered.

I was the first to arrive. I lived the closest. I found the notebook and opened it to the first page.

"I wish to see my Elna again." Underneath was written:

"I wish Eddie to have my gift. The one that is both a blessing and a curse. I wish for him to be more careful than I was about what he wishes for."

I put the notebook in my car long before anyone else got there. There was no need for anyone else to see it. I so wish I could undo that last wish of his!

It is the only thing I cannot wish for and have come true. If I write it, it happens. There are always consequences. I have experimented as he did, but even more thoroughly. If I get groceries, someone goes without. If I gain, someone loses. There is a balance in the world. Wishes simply prove it. Nothing is free.

I don't write anything down any more. Especially not lists of what I want or even what I need. I too have learned to do math in my head. I never want to discover the consequences of writing some things down.

I try not to wish at all. Sometimes I just can't help myself. I wish I could stop wishing. That too is a wish that will never be granted. So I carry on just as my grandfather did.

The pen is mightier than the sword. I'll never know why he trusted a dullard like me with a weapon like that.

About Troy Lambert

Troy Lambert works as a freelance writer and researcher by night, and the Museum Operations Specialist at the Wallace District Mining museum by day. He released the first novel in the Samuel Elijah Johnson series titled *Redemption* in April. The sequel titled *Temptation* is coming in December.

Visit Troy at his Website
http://www.troylambertwrites.com/
or at his Amazon Author Page

THE PREDATOR'S PREROGATIVE

Ira Nayman

Salah enjoys it when they run.

The blood that flows from a torn throat is warm enough, he supposes, but it is warmer when it has been coursing through an adrenaline filled body. And, it is sweeter. Perhaps the adrenaline has something to do with it. Perhaps the fear in their eyes.

"How do I look?" Salah asks Maria, his mortal consort.

She reaches over to adjust his tie. "Exquisite," she tells him.

He will feed on the ones who just stand there, paralyzed with fear, of course. A meal is a meal is a meal. But…perhaps it's just the predator's prerogative: the more your prey clings to life, the greater the pleasure you get from taking it from them. Salah does so enjoy it when they run.

"No need to wait up," Salah says. "I could be home quite late."

This is a game the two of them have played since Maria agreed to be his companion two years ago. "I shall keep that in mind," she says, even as they both know that she will be there when he returns, whenever that may be.

Salah has had many human consorts over the years;

they have, he reflects with a slight, humorless smile, 1001 uses. He sometimes wonders why they agree to work for him so willingly. He isn't especially charming, and, although perhaps exotic to look at, he doesn't consider himself particularly attractive. Perhaps they believe that if they serve him faithfully, he will make them immortal. The joke is on them, then: he wouldn't know how. Truth be told, he barely remembers how he became immortal, it happened so long ago, and nobody ever explained to him how to replicate the feat. When she has outlived her usefulness, Salah will feast on her, as he has on the consorts before her. And, like them, the last look she gives him in this life will likely be one of gratitude.

Salah gives Maria a chaste peck on the cheek. "Good hunting!" she ferociously whispers as he steps out the door of his apartment.

Salah walks out into a city of four million souls. He feels the hunger, sharp and wonderful, starting in his belly but spreading throughout his body; he hears the song of the blood calling to him. There is so much blood on the streets of the city tonight he feels light-headed with anticipation. Lurking in the shadows and feasting on human blood has been his way for as long as he can remember, and he revels in it.

Salah scouts Spadina Avenue from a nearby rooftop for a potential meal. A large Asian man walking down the street is quickly ruled out; from bitter experience he has learned that the cholesterol in the man's blood wouldn't sit well with Salah's system. The skinny young girl in the pink dress and perfect blond curls? Salah shakes his head. Girls like that might make good victims in the movies, but Salah knows that if he had her for a meal, he would be hungry an hour later.

Salah's attention falls on a couple in their early

thirties: a runty looking man walking arm in arm with a busty redhead. Yes, he thinks, you will be the appetizer and you will be the main course. The man hardly seems worth the effort, but he is wearing a garish blue shirt under a neon pink jacket; it's like he's making himself stand out from the environment specifically to get the attention of predators!

Salah follows them, silently moving from rooftop to rooftop as they walk past Chinatown Centre, past the fur stores, past Green Instead. Oh, no, he thinks to himself, they're not going to...McDonald's, are they? Seething with disgust, Salah decides that, if that turns out to be the case, he *will* eat them on general principle. But, no: before they reach the abandoned Blockbuster Video store, they cut across a parking lot. Yes, Salah thinks to himself, I like where this is going. Crossing Cameron Street, they walk into an alley.

Winning!

Salah gracefully glides from the roof of a pizza joint into the alley in front of the couple. The man looks at him with interest. The woman has a neutral expression on her face.

"I am here to feast on your blood," Salah begins his well-practiced speech. "I am your death. Run if you like - it gets the blood coursing through your veins and -"

"Really?" the man responds, a note of contempt in his voice.

"...will make it taste all the more -" Salah catches himself up short. "I'm sorry, what did you say?"

"A vampire," the man says. "Really? You expect me to believe that vampires still exist almost a decade and a half after the Singularity?"

"I am a -"

"Don't get him started," the woman interrupts.

"I will open your throat," Salah growls, "and take

pleasure in watching the blood drain from your body!"

"Pfah!" the man pfahs. "You're an anachronism! A vampire - really! What a squalid lack of imagination you must have! We live in a post-Singularity world! Do you understand what the means? All matter is computational - you could programme your body to be anything you want to be - and what do you want to be? A 'lurker in the shadows who feasts on human blood!'"

It was the scare quotes in the man's voice that really hurt Salah.

"I did warn you," the woman drily comments. "He does go on about these things."

"Allow me to introduce myself," the man says. "My name is -"

"Oh, for godless' sakes!" Salah, confused and, for the first time in a long time, worried, shouts. "I don't want to meet you - I want to EAT you!"

"Ah. The Alice dilemma," the woman placidly responds. When the two men look at her with uncomprehending gazes, she continues: "Alice is ravishingly hungry, but, when she is introduced to food, it is immediately taken away from her because in Wonderland you aren't allowed to eat things you know the name of. It would be tacky. Now, was that in *Alice's Adventures in Wonderland* or *Through the* - yikes!"

Salah, not much caring for the literary interlude, grabs the woman and pulls her towards him.

"You don't really want to be doing this," the woman advises him.

"No?" Salah responds, radiating malice. "Why not?"

The woman gestures towards the man, who has closed his eyes.

"Does your friend have narcolepsy?" Salah wonders. He prefers to dine on the flesh of the able-bodied; the lame and the sick pose no challenge. The woman is enough, he calculates, to satisfy the night's hunger.

"My friend," the woman informs him, "may be the world's foremost expert on computational matter. He can talk to atoms, you know."

"What does that matter to me?" Salah asks, pulling the woman tight with one hand while pushing back her head to expose her throat with the other. He sees that she is not afraid. Why is she not afraid? No matter - Salah will give her a slow death to punish her for her -

"If you make atoms your friend," the man answers, momentarily taking Salah's attention away from the woman, "they will do favours for you." His eyes are wide open now.

"Favours?" Salah sneers.

"You may as well let my friend go," the man tells him. "She'll be of no use to you now."

Salah thinks about this for a moment. To his surprise, he finds that he can longer hear the blood song. He is still hungry, yes, but he no longer craves human blood. Stunned, he lets the woman go; she deliberately walks over to the man's side. Salah runs his tongue over his teeth and finds that they are no longer razor sharp.

"What...happened to my incisors?" Salah asks.

"Weeelll," the man replies, "it wouldn't do to have you running around town with such formidable weapons. Somebody might get hurt."

"What," Salah gasps, beginning to grasp the severity of his situation, "what have you done to me?"

"I had a talk with the atoms in your body," the man explains. "They've been vampire atoms for a very long time. I told them that they could look forward to much more of the same if you remained a vampire. This did not please them, because atoms are always up for new experiences. I suggested that if they wanted to do new things in new objects, it might be fun for them to revert back to being normal human atoms. They agreed."

"What does that mean?" Salah moans.

"It means you're mortal again," the woman, slightly bored, tells him. She rummages around in her purse for a couple of seconds, then brings out a compact. She opens it and turns the mirror towards Salah who, for the first time in over a millennium, sees a reflection of his own young face.

"This can't be!" Salah insists. "I...I look exactly the same as I did when I was a youth - my appearance hasn't changed!"

"Why would it?" the man asks.

"My life has been sustained by unnatural means for over twelve hundred years!" Salah states. "I can't stop being a vampire without *some* consequences!"

"Oh, that," the man responds. "Well, I'm sorry, but I find the whole crumbling into dust image so cliché!"

The woman squeezes the man's arm affectionately. "Good," she says, "to see some of my aesthetic brilliance is rubbing off on you!"

"Turn me back!" Salah angrily shouts.

The man appraises him for a moment, then answers: "No."

Livid, Salah demands, "Turn! Me! Back!"

"Or, what?" the man replies. "You'll gum me to death?"

"I can still bite, you know," Salah points out.

The man shakes his head in sad disbelief. "Have you ever tasted human blood?" he asks. "As a human, I mean? Diiiiiis-gusting!"

The woman next to him frowns. "How do you know that?" she wonders.

Without taking his eyes off Salah, the man answers, "Not now, dear."

"At least, make me immortal again," Salah insists, a note of self-pity creeping into his voice.

The man and woman look at each other.

"What," the woman demands of Salah, "have you done with your...unlife?"

"I beg your pardon?" Salah, caught by surprise by the question, responds.

"Well," the woman asks, "Have you ever...written a novel?"

"Umm, no," Salah answers.

"A novelette?"

"No."

"A novella?"

"No."

"A short story?"

"No."

"A poem?"

"No."

"Not even a limerick?"

"No."

"Haiku?"

"I'm not even sure what that is."

"Umm...okay. Perhaps you...wrote a symphony?"

"No."

"Opera?"

"No."

"Violin concerto?"

"No."

"Sonata?"

"No."

"String quartet?"

"No."

"Ballad?"

"No."

"Folk song?"

"No."

"Rock song?"

"No."

"Rap song?"

"No."

"Well," the woman says, holding out her hands, "There you go, then."

Salah is confused. "What -?"

"You've been given so much time, and the best thing you could imagine doing with it is killing people and amassing fortunes - am I right? You aren't going to be given back your immortality," the woman states with finality, *"because you haven't done anything to earn it!"*

Salah is about to angrily respond when the man looks at his watch and says, "Look at the time. We really must get going if we want to have dinner in time to make the movie."

"Sorry," the woman tells Salah. "We've got to run. Plans. I'm sure you know how it is."

Without waiting for a response, the man takes the woman's arm and the pair start walking down the alley. Just before they disappear around a corner, Salah hears the woman say, "I love this city! You meet the most interesting people!"

Salah stands in the alley for several minutes, not certain what to do. The hunger in the pit of his stomach has not gone away, so he resolves that the first order of business is to get some food. Normal, human food. The woman was right, of course: he had amassed several fortunes in his many lifetimes on earth, and could probably feast on the best culinary delights the world has to offer.

But, now, right this moment, he is in immediate need of something to deal with his hunger.

All of a sudden, the McDonald's on the corner is looking like a viable option.

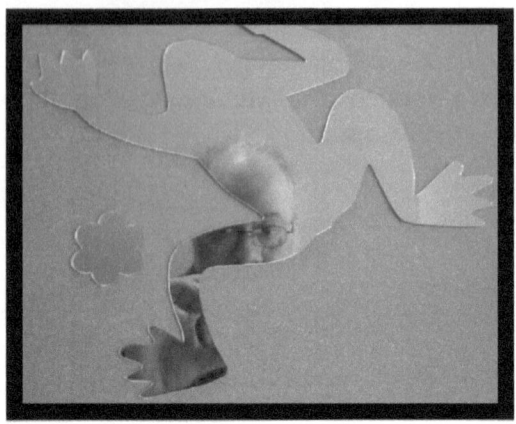

About Ira Nayman

Ira Nayman: Alternate Reality News Service (3 collections of science fiction news)...Transdimensional Authority (universe hopping novel)...Antonio Van der Whall, object psychologist (short stories)..."The Weight of Information" (radio series pilot on YouTube)...*Les Pages aux Folles* (Web page)...satirizing the world so you don't have to since 1984...

Visit Ira at his Website
http://www.lespagesauxfolles.ca/
or at his FaceBook Page

My Wife and I Argue over our Travel Plans

(Hey, I'm not Cheap but...)
Alex Carrick

I don't understand how women think. It's been a mystery to me all my life and I expect it will continue to confound me 'til the day I die.

I had a perfectly reasonable idea for how our family should spend the holidays this year.

It was practical, do-able and would have saved us a lot of money. In short, the ideal solution for what has often been a predicament in the past.

Rather than me going on like this, however, why don't I set out the discussion my wife, Donna, and I had exactly as it transpired?

Then you can decide who's was in the right.

***

DONNA: No you don't. You're not going to pull that crap again like you did last year.

ME: What do you mean? We all had a great time. Surely, you can't deny it.

DONNA: Don't call me Shirley. *(It's an old joke between us. Sadly, it's become less funny since my memory has become more spotty.)*

ME: Okay, Sweetie *(which is my way of getting around all concerns about what my wife, my kids and our pets are named)*. I had fun on that trip. And I'm pretty sure everyone else did too.

DONNA: No we did not. That's not how we wanted to see New York, taking a virtual tour by way of Google maps.

ME *(adopting an expression of mystification)*: Well I'm sorry to disagree, but I thought it was terrific. We drove around Times Square. Saw the Statue of Liberty. Took a few moments to absorb the majesty of the Brooklyn Bridge. All while staying comfortable in our living room.

DONNA: I want to go to Paris this year. Actually travel there. Not see the sights through satellite images on a computer.

ME: But then you'd have to get your hair done.

DONNA: I want to get my hair done.

ME: You'd have to buy new clothes.

DONNA: I want to buy new clothes.

ME: You'd have to learn French.

DONNA: No I wouldn't. My co-worker Rachel and her husband, Armand, went to France last year and she said they got along fine without knowing any French.

ME *(recalling Armand from an office Christmas party)*: Sure. That's because he looks like Jerry Lewis. The French love Jerry Lewis. They probably got royal treatment over there.

DONNA: That's not true. Armand doesn't look anything like Jerry Lewis. *(She stopped to consider the matter.)* Does he?

You really think so?

ME *(spotting the smallest of cracks in my wife's armor)*: Absolutely. He's the spitting image.

DONNA: Anyway, Rachel said she did most of the negotiating. She didn't find it hard. She knew enough of the language to get by and the people they met were passably good in English.

ME: She's just saying that. I know the real reason she was able to pull it off.

DONNA: Yes?

ME *(in a mumble)*: You're not going to like this.

DONNA: Go on.

ME: Well you have to admit she does bear a more than passing resemblance to Charles De Gaulle. I've been saying that for years. She has a formidable physique. *(I flexed my biceps.)* He was a national hero.

DONNA *(outraged)*: What a terrible thing to say. You'll go to any lengths to win your case. Rachel is a lovely woman. There's real character in her face.

ME *(mumbling some more)*: Or Gerard Depardieu. She could be Gerard Depardieu's twin sister. You know, the actor who played Cyrano de Bergerac in the movie.

DONNA: Stop it. You do this all the time. You hijack our arguments with some crazy point and then you get your way. Not this time, buster.

ME *(changing tack)*: I love logging onto Google maps. You can see anything and go anywhere. It's so neat.

DONNA: Yes, that's true. But I want to actually sit in a café on the Champs Elysees. It's been my fondest dream all my life.

ME: I want to visit Paris too, but in a better way.

DONNA: You've already been there, old-fashioned style. I know it's not as high a priority for you. It was part of your European tour one summer while you were in university.

ME: Exactly. And I remember some things you wouldn't like.

DONNA: Such as?

ME: There were rude waiters. Lots and lots of rude waiters.

DONNA: Like we haven't encountered that right here at home, often because you've stiffed them on the tip.

ME: They'll insult us in French over there.

DONNA: So let me get this straight. I won't understand what they're saying. But they'll be gesturing with Gallic flare. *(A smile lit up her face.)* Sounds romantic to me.

ME *(conceding the point and moving on)*: We'd all have to get medical shots. There are savages in Paris.

DONNA: No way.

ME: And pestilence. Big, big mosquitoes. Trés grandes mosquitoes.

DONNA: Again, no way, monsieur. You're making this stuff up.

ME: Better to view the sights from our own couch.

DONNA: Uh-uh. The kids need the culture. They can see

the Mona Lisa in the Louvre. The works of the impressionists in the Musée d'Orsay.

ME: We can look them up on-line.

DONNA: They can walk under the Arc de Triomphe. Visit Napoleon's tomb. Stroll the boulevards. Sit in the Tuileries Gardens.

ME: How do you know all this stuff? *(My wife can be awesome when she sets her mind to a challenge. That's why I have to be nimble on my mental feet. Mental feet? Does that seem in any way correct?)*

DONNA: I've done my research. On-line, I might add. That's what you use the Internet for. Not to go on some pretend trip.

ME *(changing tack once again)*: Remember when you wanted to go back to your old homestead in Saskatchewan and see how much things had changed?

DONNA: Yes. I do. That was another fiasco.

ME: How can you say that? We looked up the address on Google's search engine and went for a make-believe drive.

Donna was starting to appear really upset. I knew I was on thin ice, but kept skating anyway.

ME: We headed down the street you used to take when you walked home from school. Then there it was – the site of your old house. Now it's just an empty lot. Remember how disappointed you were.

DONNA: I can't believe I'm saying this, but you're right.

ME: Imagine if we'd gone there in person. It would have been so much more of a shock.

DONNA: Where are you taking this?

ME: Well it's the same with Paris. We'll get packed. Hop on a plane. Find a hotel room. Put on our walking shoes. And then we'll discover the Eiffel Tower's been replaced by a Walmart.

DONNA *(giving me one of her disgusted looks)*: Don't be ridiculous. That would never happen.

ME: They have a Disneyland over there, you know. I'm not entirely sure, but I think I heard it was built on the site of Notre Dame Cathedral.

DONNA: What nonsense. You pull this stunt and the kids will sit around the computer looking surly as can be.

ME: Are you kidding me? They're teenagers. We could go halfway around the world and they'd still look surly most of the time. At least my way, we'll save thousands of dollars.

DONNA: Ah-hah! Now we're coming to the crux of the matter. This is all about money. You're so cheap, you don't want to pay for this trip.

ME: I'm just thinking of the family. There are so many better ways we could spend our incomes. Like on golf lessons. *(A pause to appreciate how bad that sounded.)* For you and the kids, I mean.

DONNA: Listen up, Mister Miser. We're going on this trip, whether you like the idea or not. So get out your credit card and let's go online. But not for any lame vacation in cyberspace. Rather to book an airline and a hotel.

ME: Really? Do we have to?

DONNA: Yes we have to. And there'll be a whole lot more

inconvenience for you and me and the kids before we're finished.

ME *(looking truly apprehensive)*: I know. There's the time spent in airports and taxi cabs. Plus the days away from my job. I'm very busy at work these days, you know.

DONNA: Oh for goodness sakes, you need a holiday. You're not Iron Man.

She had a point. Lately I've been feeling less like Iron Man and more like Putty Man.

DONNA: Plus don't leave out the strange food. And the time difference. But it will be fantastic just the same.

I was looking more and more appalled.

DONNA: Being your wife and nurturing this family has taught me many wonderful things. I believe I've become a zen master on the subject of the human condition.

My discomfort was stacking up like pommes frites. I was becoming the croissant smothered under fromage.

DONNA: And do you know what the most important lesson of all is?

ME: No. Do tell.

DONNA *(with mischief in her eyes)*: That most of the time you have to be miserable in this life to be happy.

About Alex Carrick

Alex Carrick has been a professional economist covering the construction industry for the past thirty-nine years. He writes extensively on economic matters for several newsletters, newspapers and the Internet, dealing with both Canada and the United States. Mr. Carrick lives in Toronto, Canada and is married with three children. A lethargic dog and crazy cat round out the household.

Visit Alex at his Website
http://www.alexcarrick.com/
or at his Amazon Author Page

Oh, Okay, and the Good Soldier Schweik

(Fort Drum, New York 1980)

John Thompson

Jaroslav Hasek's famous novel *The Good Soldier Schweik* concerns a simple-minded soldier in the Austro-Hungarian Army of 1914, who is subversive in his simplicity.

Given an order, he does his best to understand it (but seldom does) and then does his best to comply with what he understands -- usually in a way that fails completely. Hidden under the simplicity is an even simpler idea, Schweik prefers life on his own terms and not those of the Army.

For some unimaginable reason *The Good Soldier Schweik* was firmly banned from the barracks of several European armies.

In the Army, there are orders and there are *Orders*. There are also leaders and *Leaders*. It takes some time to distinguish between the two.

There are orders that must be obeyed. The recruit learns how to do so on the drill square, and later learns not to question simple commands like "Come here". Direct orders like "Go sweep out the vehicle bays" leave little room for ambivalence and the young recruit might confine himself to asking where the brooms are kept. It is also unquestionably easy to obey any order, because everyone outranks the recruit.

The young soldier eventually gets to know bit about the chain of command . He might politely query an order like "You three come with me" if it is delivered by an unfamiliar Warrant Officer while he is under supervision of his own Sergeant. Likewise, as a callow young officer, I eventually learned that directly detailing privates to do something when I should have asked their Sergeant for "volunteers" was a sure road to chaos.

After a while, it dawns on a soldier that the Army is never a smoothly functioning team save when it is well rehearsed in familiar tasks. The unfamiliar observer might marvel at the quick hive of activity that is the deployment of an artillery battery, the rolling smoothness of a squadron forming into a laager, or the precision of an infantry battalion marching in review. But the young soldier heard the argumentative radio-traffic, learned about who got lost, and watched the quartermaster tearing his hair out by the roots.

A soldier soon becomes a very keen judge of competence and ability. He may even become a perverse connoisseur of incompetence, appreciating the way young 2Lt Maladroit doesn't yet know his "arse from a hole in the ground, but seems to be learning fast" while dreading the ability of Major Retentive to fixate on the trivial while ignoring the important. Hopefully, the Major's interference might provoke another fine display of auto-depilatory behavior by Quartermaster Sergeant Stubblefield.

As it goes for the private, so it goes for the young officer. There are orders and there are *Orders*; there are leaders and there are *Leaders*. Hopefully, the *Orders* come from the *Leaders*, but most of these are more likely to give orders –usually trusting in your common-sense and intelligence to see things through. Surprisingly, this often works. It tends to be the leaders who give *Orders*; often because they want you to do something they wouldn't do themselves, or because they still think that forceful delivery can compensate for their own shortcomings.

Eventually, the experienced soldier learns to follow the orders, and subvert the *Orders* when necessary. He respects and admires the *Leaders*, and endures the leaders while quietly seeking to limit their authority over him under any circumstances.

Bart was one of my closest friends when we were subalterns together. Bart is a gentle soul, erudite and possessed of a calm humour. Currently, he is one of our diplomats and his gifts seem to stand him in good stead. His career seems to be prospering in spite of, or perhaps because of, his one principle of insubordination that he learned in the Army.

Bart is one of the few people who are better read than I am and introduced me to the *Good Soldier Schweik* and to Norm Dixon's classic study *The Psychology of Military Incompetence*. The latter has universal application for anal-retentive conformists are attracted to any environment with a hierarchical structure. It is just that in a military, as opposed to the civil service or a major corporation, incompetence can be as glaringly obvious. As a military is seldom properly used in peacetime, the anal retentive conformists can be quite common.

Bart's solution to leaders with *Orders* was to adopt the "Oh, Okay" school of compliance. He would cheerfully strive to obey directions to the point where things were about to fail and then report back for more directions. This usually let the leader feel involved in the whole process. In the meantime, he would do everything possible to salvage manpower and resources from the impending wreck and insulate his subordinates from his errant superior. Bart's men soon had a strong affection for him.

"Oh, Okay" saw Bart through a lot -- including a couple of weeks under my inexpert guidance during a major exercise on an American military base. Our Reconnaissance Squadron was getting up to full strength in terms of manpower, but was rich in talented young officers.

Being fresh from my Lieutenant's qualification course, I was lusting for my own reconnaissance troop. Instead, I was saddled with the Assault Troop. Ideally, this is a group of about five small teams of expert troopers who handle a number of small tasks that that the scout cars can't handle. In practice, we stuffed it full of half-trained troopers who had yet to properly learn how to drive jeeps, master radio voice-procedure, or work a machine-gun. As all the trained corporals and other young NCOs were otherwise employed, I was given a couple of drivers and Bart -- fresh from his Second Lieutenant Qualification courses -- to act as my deputy.

As a Recce Squadron is normally far out in front of the regular battle groups and combat teams, it seldom really integrates with them all that well. As a result, we were frequently tasked to act as the enemy force on large exercises. This meant that we could both hone our own skills and have all the fun. Our guys embraced being "Fantasians" -- the vaguely Soviet-like enemy force. Thanks to some expert scrounging and a small group of friendly American Green-Berets, we all ended up carrying Soviet-style soldier's identity books and wearing the insignia of our Warsaw Pact opposite numbers. Bogus accents blossomed and our own strong sense of élan -soared to new levels.

There is a downside to being the enemy force. Exercises are often scripted, and the directing staff (or DS) is usually around to make sure encounters unfold as they should, so that they can judge the results. The blue-side is not so closely supervised -- there might be one DS with a company of infantry. The red-side tends to have many more. My assault troop was saddled with an ex-Regimental Sergeant Major, a man with almost thikrty years of soldiering (in another regiment from ours) under his belt. To make things worse, Mr. Lensmen and I did not take to each other from the start. While being civil to each other there was an underlying tension between us.

The exercise got off to an excellent start -- the Blue Force was slow and unwieldy, while the forte of a Reconnaissance squadron is speed and decisiveness. Their logistics train was still moving into place under a weak rearguard when we pounced. Hamish, one of our troop commanders, achieved a measure of distinction when his troop snapped up a medical company commanded by his equally eccentric father. His shout of "Hands up, everybody -- you too, Dad!" was certainly one for the record books.

My part did not go so well... We suspected an anti-tank detachment lay in wait for our scout cars to appear, and I led a fighting patrol out to see if we could snap it up. We were creeping along in fine-style, crawling up ditches, and creeping through the bracken. Mr. Lensmen, possessed of the gravity of a very senior NCO and being thirty years older than us, paced leisurely along beside the patrol. The pair of Jeep-mounted 106mm Recoilless Rifle crews did not see us, but did see a member of the DS walking towards them.

They came to a natural conclusion and called down a mortar shoot on us, whereupon Mr. Lensmen was informed of the shoot over his radio on the DS frequency.

He then consulted his map, determined that the rain of imaginary 81mm mortar bombs was coming exactly down on our heads, and informed me that half of my patrol (and me) were now casualties. There was no appeal, and so I settled down to the two-hour nap of the exercise "dead".

To be perfectly fair to Mr. Lensmen, crawling and creeping about is a very strenuous activity even for eighteen-year old privates and twenty-one-year-old officers. A fifty-year-old man cannot be expected to keep up. I took him aside and politely suggested that next time he might wish to remain a hundred meters or so behind us or under cover. He said that he would think about it. The next day we all settled into another two hour nap as Mr. Lensmen was disinclined to slither through a swamp; preferring to walk around it in full view of a company of infantry.

Strictly speaking, a senior Chief Warrant Officer doesn't outrank a newly minted Lieutenant. Practically speaking, the Lieutenant had better not get in a pissing contest with one -- someone is going to lose and it won't be the NCO. For all practical purposes, I was clearly outranked on those occasions where it was necessary to butt heads.

We were lying up late one afternoon, preparing for a series of patrols and probing attacks on the Blue Force, when Bart approached me. Mr. Lensmen was napping in the back of our truck, but the Directing Staff radio had been left on, and was sitting unattended elsewhere in our Hide. Bart, accidentally and not on purpose, had been eavesdropping and learned that the same Anti-tank detachment we had been after two days earlier was in the neighborhood. Moreover, the DS who was with them was fairly certain that the 106s would bag the first couple of scout-cars to exit our Hide.

Likewise accidentally and not on purpose, I left Mr. Lensmen where he was dozing and meandered over to a spot where it would be hypothetically possible to spot the anti-tank team. Then I called in a Contact Report to Squadron Headquarters and received permission to try and capture them with another fighting patrol. One was swiftly organized, but alas, the napping Mr. Lensman was inadvertently left behind as we departed.

Perhaps this was just as well. In my eagerness to close with the team, I acted with more haste than care and the sortie turned into a debacle. The Blue Force caught us flat-footed and this time it was my fault. At least Mr. Lensmen was not there to witness my humiliation but he did have a lot to say on my return. Moreover, the Chief of the Directing Staff had a few words with my Squadron Commander who also had a few choice words with me.

Accidentally and not on purpose, the Directing Staff decided that it was high time some prisoners were taken in the exercise. Being "killed" meant a two-hour reprise and the quiet shame of knowing that had the exercise been real warfare, you'd have really screwed things up. Being captured meant a night or so in the kind and loving hands of the Intelligence Cell, which had no sense of hospitality but did have a lovely program to induce a one-way flow of information. Mr. Lensmen informed me that I should lead the patrol, and that on no account was I to leave him behind this time.

It was time for the "Oh, Okay" School of obedience.

That evening, we went in by truck to a hide some four kilometers in front of the Blue-Force's forward infantry companies. I then went ahead to scout out the initial part of the route we would take. As Mr. Lensmen was sticking to me like glue. I took pains to make this a difficult route. When we returned, I announced there would be enough time for a couple of hours of sleep. This was not solicitude so much as it was cruelty. Give a man thirty to forty-five minutes or so to sleep, and it's a nap. Give him something more than that but wake him up before four hours (and a full sleep cycle) have passed, and he has to fight back to wakefulness and remains much groggier than he normally would.

Mr. Lensmen curled up in a sleeping-bag liner under a ground sheet. So did most of my other lads except for the trio that I selected to come on the patrol. Bart was also going forward with another trio to be a security element for my group as we went in. The rest of the Assault Troop was snoring away. As it came time for my departure, the most Schweikesque portion of my plan was executed.

In any group of soldiers, there will be one dull, lazy and stupid one who thinks he is just clever enough to lie to you. I had ensured that our example would be the sentry in the half-hour before my patrol left. I sent Buggins around to wake up Mr. Lensmen, secure in the knowledge that he would never dare to shake a Chief Warrant Officer awake, but would lie to me about trying to do so. This is exactly what happened -- in front of witnesses too. Being naturally preoccupied with my final preparations, I sent Buggins out to ensure Mr. Lensmen was up three times. Three times Buggins came back and said that he had done so. The minutes ticked by, and there was no sign of our DS.

Then it was time to depart and I cheerfully told Buggins to let Mr. Lensmen know what direction we had departed in. Behaving in this manner can -- deservedly -- land you in very hot water. However, if you pull off a coup, much will be forgiven.

My original intent was to crawl in and drag off an enemy prisoner as fodder for the Intelligence Cell (they were neutral in this exercise and would eagerly interrogate anyone who was delivered to them). Instead, as we crawled towards the selected company, I heard the distant sound of an electrical generator. In a battalion area, generators are usually only found with the Headquarters unit -- which constantly needs power for its radios and work area. There was a quick change of plan and we homed in the sound.

As we neared the HQ area, their sentries made life easy for us. Secure in the knowledge that they were three kilometers to the rear of the line of entrenched infantry companies, one was smoking and chatting to his companion. We easily slid by them, and found ourselves right by the HQ vehicles. I was a bundle of excitement -- there were so many exciting targets at four am for a thunderflash (which simulates grenades) and magazine or two of 9mm blank ammunition that I hardly knew where to begin. However, Trooper Read made up my mind for me. I heard a glugging sound, and spotted Read swallowing the better part of a pitcher of lemonade left by the hood of a command post van.

When a Headquarters is laying out refreshments it means that an orders group was imminent. An O-Group is where all the main subordinate commanders and the representatives of the supporting arms are given their instructions. Naturally, there may be printed signal operating instructions (SOI) for the day -- code-words, frequencies, etc. There might be copies of the orders written down, and there certainly will be a trace -- the sketched transparent overlay on the map that details positions, axis of advance, obstacle belts, artillery fire-plans, and much, much more.

I scooped the SOI into my pocket, grabbed the trace and map-board and relieved Read of the rest of the lemonade. We scuttled off into the darkness, slipped by their oblivious sentries again and then ran snickering into the last hour of the night.

About twenty minutes later, a series of parachute flares shot up from the HQ we had just plundered, and from the infantry companies in front of us. We soon found out that the entire enemy force was spitting out improvised patrols in all directions too. Fortunately Bart was in a position to occupy the attention of the company athwart our exit route and we slipped by to a hasty rendezvous with Hamish.

Mr. Lensmen was livid with me in that fire and ice way that Chief Warrant Officers reserve for bouncy young subalterns. However, my stock was suddenly very high with my squadron commander and my whole Regiment, and the DS radio net was too crowded with messages about the sudden accuracy of Red-Force artillery fire for any complaints to be forwarded. As for the Intelligence Cell folks, they had been sitting in with the Battalion Headquarters waiting to receive some prisoners (to wit, me and my patrol) when they saw us sneak into the HQ and steal their maps. This gave them fodder for lectures on security and the threat of Spetsnaz for some years to come. It also gave me a leg-up for an interesting posting when it was time for my staff-tour a few years later.

A couple of years later, Bart and I were discussing a superior officer who neither of us much respected. Bart mentioned that it was time for the "Oh-Okay" school of compliance to come into effect. I told him I had always admired his notion of creative obedience and asked him when he first put it together. Some questions are best left un-asked. "Having to put up with you," he replied.

About John Thompson

John Thompson was born into a Canadian Air Force family in 1959, served in the Canadian Army for thirteen years, and was a researcher and commentator with the Canadian Institute of Strategic Studies and Mackenzie Institute from 1985 to the present. He currently still sits on the officer's association of his old regiment and is a member of the Royal Canadian Military Institute.

Look for his critically acclaimed chronology of WWII:
Spirit Over Steel

We hope you have enjoyed this cross-genre anthology,
brought to you by

CARRICK PUBLISHING

Visit us at
http://www.carrickpublishing.com/